SIX SILVER BULLETS

For Sheriff Bruce Harrington the mystery of the legendary Robin Hood figure known as *El Matador* became mingled with the much less mythical highway robbery of an army payroll. Before he had finished his investigation however, he was a lot less certain that *El Matador* was a myth, even once he *knew* that *El Matador* had nothing to do with the robbery.

GEORGE FLYNN

SIX SILVER BULLETS

E.P.L. - SPW

Complete and Unabridged

LINFORD
Leicester

First published in Great Britain in 1990 by
Robert Hale Limited
London

First Linford Edition
published October 1992
by arrangement with
Robert Hale Limited
London

British Library CIP Data

Flynn, George
Six silver bullets.—Large print ed.—
Linford western library
I. Title II. Series
823.914 [F]

ISBN 0–7089–7254–3

Published by
F. A. Thorpe (Publishing) Ltd.
Anstey, Leicestershire

Set by Words & Graphics Ltd.
Anstey, Leicestershire
Printed and bound in Great Britain by
T. J. Press (Padstow) Ltd., Padstow, Cornwall

1

Disturbing Times

IT was one of those stories that insidiously spread, and in which substance appeared to be founded less on facts which could be substantiated than upon myths and superstitions which could not. While the superstition was not limited to the Mexican population of Camargo, the truth lay somewhere between the legend and the fact.

There was a person known as *El Matador* — The Killer — but he had not lived any hundred years and did not appear out of the dusk as *El Visitador* — The Visitor — to take from the rich and give to the poor. Or did he?

Nor did he appear on a black horse, a lean, expressionless man attired in black wearing a Colt sidearm with ivory grips who, after completing his mission of punishing the greedy, the exploiters, disappeared, even in broad daylight.

However, it supported the faith and the hope of the 'pantless ones' that although their fathers and grandfathers had known of him — had upon occasion actually seen him — as Bruce Harrington, sheriff of sparsely inhabited Coyotero County of southern New Mexico Territory had said several times, *El Matador* certainly existed, but his deeds had only been known to be the work of a particular phantom within the last fifteen or so years. He also stated drily that fifteen years was not an extraordinary period of time for *fantasma* to exist.

Sheriff Harrington was a large, powerful man in his late thirties whose reputation for maintaining order in his bailiwick was well known even beyond Coyotero County. But his pronouncements against some legendary gunman dressed in black riding a black horse and carrying an ivory-stocked sixgun, while rarely openly questioned in his presence, were nonetheless disagreed with among some of the late-comers — the *norte americanos* — of the south desert.

Their largely mute conviction was reinforced the early spring of the same year a colonel, brevet brigadier general, suicidally attacked five thousand northern Indians with only a few hundred men, no artillery, and caused the halt of all commercial and industrial activity nationwide when the horror of his débâcle became known. Custer's 'Massacre'.

The nation's newspapers were filled with lurid tales of scalping, maiming, plundering, of an incredible slaughter.

When the story of this stunning defeat reached the South Desert, it may have been inevitable that, once again, *El Matador* should appear. There were a number of reasons put forth for him to appear at this time. Some were probably fairly accurate; most were either hysterically ridiculous or founded in the inherent fear of Indian raiders who still occasionally ran wild north of the border and whose depredations were both legendary and solidly rooted in historical fact. If the American Army had been butchered up north by Indians, who could say another such massing of tribesmen was not in progress, perhaps down in Mexico where US soldiers could not go? Who could say such a fierce bloodletting was not about to descend upon Camargo?

Sheriff Bruce Harrington for one, said it was not possible in the southern territory. There were too many army posts, camps and stations and too few Indians left to do more than mount lightning-like raids, usually to steal horses. He said Mexican border-jumpers were far more likely to ride in screaming waves, brandishing weapons, bellies full of tequila or pulque.

That statement did little to lessen the fear, nor was it ever claimed that Bruce Harrington was a man of tact.

4

What finally did happen, occurred on one of those flawlessly magnificent early springtime days. Three stage coaches left Raton up north within two hours of one another, the first one carrying no passengers, only light freight, the second one carrying heavily armed professional shootists. Slightly less than two hours later the third coach appeared in the dust. None of those coaches had outriders, which would have told anyone watching that valuable cargo was aboard. Later, Sheriff Harrington swore in exasperation saying — truthfully — that if there had been outriders the attack probably would not have occurred or, if it had, it would not have been a surprise.

North of Camargo where the road dipped into one of those erosion gullies which carried off the infrequent, usually torrential downpours, the first and second stages had no difficulty nor did the sharp-eyed drivers, gunguards and shootists see anything out of the ordinary, and again probably because the attribute of hindsight was always better than foresight, Sheriff Harrington profanely denounced the idea of having those coaches two hours apart. They should have been tailgate to tailgate, he said, and again, he was probably correct.

When the third stage swept up over the crest of the swale, the horses set back against their britchings, the whip had slack lines in his hands and the solitary gunguard yelled to a man inside the coach.

"Roadblock, Henry!"

Before the driver got his hitch stopped there was not a shred of doubt in anyone's mind that, since the first two, decoy, stages had passed this precise spot some time earlier, obviously having encountered no obstacle of huge boulders, what they were facing now was an unmistakable, man-made road block whose purpose was simply to halt the stage-coach carrying the newly-minted money to the scattering of army posts down along the border.

Later, during Sheriff Harrington's conference with stage company officials he said, "Whoever among you gents put the money-coach last is responsible. It should have been in the middle, for Chrissake."

It wasn't in the middle. In fact those scheduled two-hour intervals were as much at fault for what happened as anything else.

The whip and gunguard, on their high seat, sat like stones, eyes rummaging the underbrush, rocks, little interspersed clearings. He was out there. Maybe more than one, in which case *they* were out there and the pair of men on the high seat were totally vulnerable, which was why neither of them moved. The gunguard had a Winchester across his lap. Both he and the driver wore sidearms.

The heavily-armed man inside gripped his carbine and flattened back out of sight. He could be the bravest soul on earth, but unless he was also a fool he would not fight to protect the bullion

7

boxes if there were more than one of them out there waiting and watching.

Dust was settling when a man called ahead. "Throw down the guns!"

The whip, sweating like a stud-horse, flung away his sixgun and growled at the gunguard to do the same. He was obeyed but with obvious reluctance. He was young — twenty-one — and this was his first run as a gunguard. It would also probably be his last. He flung the guns away with a bitter curse.

The voice called again, unhurried, calm enough to have been engaging in casual conversation. "You inside! Pitch 'em out the window."

The inside guard was older, tougher, more seasoned.

"Come an' get 'em," he called back, and the reaction to his challenge sailed through the air to land a few feet from the stage coach. It was about ten inches long, was wrapped in red waxed paper and had a short fuse protruding from one end.

8

The voice called again. "You inside! You, got five seconds. The next stick will have a lighted fuse."

On the high seat the whip, an older man, stared in horror at the small red object and called to the man inside.

"Throw 'em out, Henry, for Chrissake."

A shotgun, a Winchester and a sixgun were hurled from below.

The calm voice gave another order. "The three of you get down, place the bullion boxes at the edge of the road, then go roll those boulders out of the way. *Move!* Your friends will miss you soon. *Move or I'll blow you to hell.*"

They moved. Each of three steel-bound sturdy little boxes were laboriously carried to the edge of the road without another word being spoken. When that had been accomplished and the whip, an older man, straightened up with hands on his hips to brace backwards in order to relieve back pain, his companions mopped off sweat as they headed for the rocks. Some of them required all three men to move, but it was eventually done and the calm voice which came from the west side of the road, but which could have come from any direction over there, said, "*Adios, muchachos*. Get it moving and keep it moving!"

The whip kicked off his binders, whistled up his hitch and looked morosely past the head of his leaders as the vehicle began to move again. Beside him the youthful gunguard said, "There was only one, Matt."

The older man did not look around. "How do you know? There was only one man tellin' us what to do. For all you know there could have ten more hiding in the underbush."

". . . At least he wasn't a Mex. No accent."

The whip closed his mouth and concentrated on reaching Camargo. He swore to himself about half the way. No one told him how much was in those boxes, but if it was the payroll for more than one of those border outposts it had to be more than he'd make if he lived to be a hundred and fifty. And it wasn't his fault that he'd lost it, but telling company officials that would be about as likely to produce appreciable results as peeing in the ocean.

When he slackened off on the final pull into Camargo there was another coach turning back on the outskirts. It was the one full of shootists and that moved the unhappy whip to growl to the youth beside him. "Look yonder; here comes the war-wagon." He said a foul word that rang with scorn. "Why didn't they put one crate in each of the damned coaches?"

The gunguard said nothing. He had worked three years as a corralyard hostler waiting for just one chance to advance. The opportunity had come, he had settled himself for the long drive with a Winchester between his knees, a sixgun on his hip, a sawed-off scattergun at his feet in the front boot, and a .41 under and-over bellygun in his waistband.

Those older men, hardened shootists

to a man, would listen to his excuses and laugh in his face, which was not hard to do when they'd been entering Camargo before deciding to turn back. They hadn't seen the boulders in the road nor that stick of dynamite.

The whip was too disgusted to reply to the shouts of the armed men in the other stage. He did not even look in their direction as he tooled his vehicle down the centre of the wide, dusty roadway, turned in at the company corralyard, kicked on the binders, hurled the lines to a waiting Mexican yardman and climbed down hand over hand to face three dusty individuals in matching coats and britches who watched solemn as owls as the whip reached the ground and turned on them with a bitter expression. "Lost it, gents. Back up where the big swale was."

Of the three horrified stage company executives only the youngest found his tongue. "How?"

The whip was pulling off his gloves when he replied: "Boulders in the road.

Rolled out there after the load of gunfighters went past, before I could get close enough to see down into that swale."

A fiercely-moustached bull-necked older man, red as a beet, said, "Why didn't you go around?"

"Didn't have the footage, Mister Brant. I was comin' down over the crest and — hell — there it was. No way at the bottom of the swale to — ."

"Gawda'mighty damn! Matt . . . how many was there?"

"One called the orders. I didn't see him nor the others — if there was others hid out through the underbrush."

Mister Brant turned an apopletic face toward the youthful gunguard. "What in the tarnation hell do you think we hired you to do? Set up there like a gawddamned bump on a log?"

The youth could not speak. The whip said, "Mister Brant, there wasn't a damned thing he could have done. We was targets. If he'd done somethin' foolish he'd likely have got me shot too. I told him to throw down his weapons."

Sheriff Harrington appeared in the yard. He had already heard of the robbery from several of the shootists over in the saloon. They laughed about it. Harrington was not amused but he understood how hired gunmen would be — men like bull-necked, fierce Charles Brant, president of the stage company were held in cordial contempt. They paid money, took no risks, and in the event of something going wrong, paid for no funerals.

When Brant was wheeling on the gunguard again Sheriff Harrington walked up and said, "What goddamned fool planned this stunt?"

Brant recoiled, eyes unwaveringly hostile. Behind him the other two company men were expressionless and mute, but it seemed that one of them had a sardonic twinkle in his eyes.

"I did," roared the heavy-set older man turning on the sheriff, "There

14

wasn't anything wrong with it, except that — "

"Except that you had the bullion coach last when it should have been in the middle, and except that only a fool would load three boxes into one stage, and finally because — "

"Who the hell do you think you're talking to?" roared the older man, and got back an immediate response.

"Whoever planned that mess. You — if you planned it."

"You're the sheriff? Well, do you know who I am?"

Harrington shook his head. "No, I don't. But I'll tell you who *I* am; I'm the lucky devil who has got to ride his butt raw trying to find what became of those boxes, and I wouldn't have to do that if you'd done your job right in the first place."

Harrington went over to the corral-yard office. Behind him two Mexican hostlers who were taking horses off the stage's tongue were leaning over almost strangling to keep from laughing.

Albert Brant's swollen neck and angry eyes did not leave Harrington's walking form until the office door closed behind him. Then Brant turned on the other two company officials.

His rage was awesome. He roared that now they'd lose government contracts, probably lose the mail-hauling franchises as well. The company's reputation would be ruined and it was the fault of his advisers. He should fire every last one of them — and — that upstart of a beardless gunguard, his defender the stage driver, and when all that had been cared for, he should concentrate on breaking the sheriff of Coyotero County for daring to speak to him as he had.

2

Three Riders

THE whip and two of the hired gunmen were slouching along the bar when Sheriff Harrington walked in. They saw him enter, as did other customers as well as the overweight saloonman behind the bar. He, at least, had a valid excuse for turning away; he was fishing glasses out of a bucket of greasy water and drying them. He at least, was occupied.

The gunmen, leaning like crows on a fence looked into a backbar mirror while toying with their drinks, but Matt Wales, the whip Charles Brant had bellowed at, finished his drink and slowly turned as Sheriff Harrington settled further down the bar. Preliminaries were unnecessary, the same topic was on everyone's mind. "Wasn't a damned thing the lad nor I could do," he said. "And that feller inside — if he'd got raunchy he'd have got us all blown to hell."

Harrington nodded as the poker-faced barman set a beer in front of him and walked away as Harrington gazed at the driver, whom he knew, not well, but casually. "How big was those rocks in the road?" he asked mildly.

Matt wagged his head. "Big enough. Took me'n the lad and the guard inside to roll each one out of the way."

Sheriff Harrington saw the hefty barman gazing at him. He winked and the hefty man winked back. Then Harrington made a quiet statement which attracted the attention of the others, including the hired gunmen. "Wouldn't have been one man then, would it?"

Matt Wales's eyes widened, and he smiled. "That's right. By gawd I done the right thing."

Sheriff Harrington showed a wintry small smile as he reached for the beer

18

glass. "Yeah. Without knowing it."

The whip straightened up off the bar and was turning as he said, "I'm goin' to find Mister Brant and — "

"Leave it be for now," the lawman said, drank half the glass and was putting it aside when he finished. "Who is Mister Brant?"

"Head of the stage company. I'd only seen him once or twice since I been tooling stages for the company. I think he pretty much runs things from up in Denver. That's company headquarters . . . When I saw him get on one of the stages, with his friends, the other fellers in suits and little curly-brimmed derby hats, I told the lad settin' beside me, it had to be somethin' real important to get him all the way down here to ride with the bullion crates.

One of those indolent-acting gunmen smiled down the bar at Sheriff Harrington. "Nice gent, ain't he?"

Harrington ignored that to ask the whip another question. "Before you pulled out did anyone suggest to Mister

Brant that the money-coach should be in the middle and the coaches strung out closer together?"

Matt Wales rolled his eyes. "Mister Harrington, don't anyone ever say somethin' like that to Charles Brant. I've heard enough stories about him durin' the six years I been driving for the company to know that for a fact."

That smiling gunman farther up the bar spoke again, still showing a hint of a sardonic smile. "I've rode guard for him before. Quite a few times in fact, sometimes inside, sometimes as an outrider. Couple times I rode inside with him. Special occasions. Sheriff, the driver's right: You don't make suggestions and you don't criticise — you just listen an' when he tells you somethin' you nod your head." The gunguard gazed into his little empty jolt glass before continuing. "He's sure a mile from bein' perfect. I've seen him do things just as foolish as this, and I only once heard a feller tellin' him that he done wrong, and the next day I helped that feller saddle up and watched him ride out. The pay's good, Sheriff, the rest of it's none of anyone's business but the head In'ian."

Bruce Harrington eyed the speaker, who was a youngish man with pale eyes and hair who dressed well and wore his holstered gun low and tied down. The man had not spoken as though he had just given Harrington a warning, but it had still come down to that.

The lawman said, "You're wrong, friend. It's everyone's business, beginnin' with me who's got to put on a tin bill and get down an' scratch with the chickens tryin' to find that money. It's the army's business because if that was a payroll, and I understand it was, a lot of soldiers aren't goin' to be real happy. And it's the business of you an' everyone like you who didn't tell Mister Brant what he was doing was somethin' a ten-year-old kid would know better'n to do."

Sheriff Harrington turned his attention

back to the driver. "You never saw him?"

"Nope. He was hid."

"What was his voice like?"

"No accent, didn't sound like a Messican . . . Calm voice; never yelled, only when he gave an order, an' even then he didn't yell — he just made it sound like a person had better obey."

Sheriff Harrington finished his beer and returned to the roadway where little groups of people stood here and there discussing the most recent cause for excitement. What he did not know until he saw the poster over on the corralyard gate, was that the stage company was offering a one thousand dollar reward for information about the money-crates and the outlaw, or outlaws, who had taken them at gun point. The hand-lettered poster was signed by Charles Brant.

Sheriff Harrington gave the bull-necked, fierce tempered old man credit for one thing: he didn't waste any time.

That pale-eyed, pale-haired, lean younger man who had spoken at the saloon walked into the jailhouse office as unruffled as he'd acted up at the bar. He smiled, too, which he seemed to do easily, invited himself to use a chair, tipped back his hat and eyed the larger, burlier and older man at the desk.

"You goin' to get up a posse?" he asked quietly, and met Sheriff Harrington's irritable glare without losing his smile. "Because if you are, I'd like to ride along."

Harrington nodded woodenly. "It's a big reward," he said drily. "Biggest I've ever heard of in the south desert country."

The pale-eyed man got more comfortable before speaking again. "It's downright respectable, Sheriff. Well . . . ?"

"What's your name?"

"Bryce Hadley. First name don't sound a lot different from yours, does it?"

Sheriff Harrington did not answer the question, which did not actually require an answer. He instead asked another question. "How about your friends, they want to ride along too?"

Hadley shrugged. "I doubt it. We got paid for goin' and coming. Last I heard up at the bar, they want to collect in full so they'll take the next stage north, along with Mister Brant."

"Why don't you go with them?" Harrington asked, and got that gentle smile again. "For one thousand reasons, Sheriff."

Harrington stood up. "All right. You got a Winchester?"

"Yes."

"Meet you down at the livery barn in fifteen minutes."

The tall, lean man arose and without another word returned to the roadway leaving Bruce Harrington standing there looking after him for a moment or two. From gunguard to bounty-hunter within about an hour. Well, Mister Hadley was going to learn something

24

about the law in the south desert country. There would not be a posse.

On his way up to his room at the hotel Sheriff Harrington encountered Matt Wales standing morosely in front of the stage company office. Harrington said, "Fired?"

Matt nodded. "Both of us, me'n the lad. I been standin' here wonderin' how long I'd stay in jail if I walked back in there and knocked Brant's nose sideways."

Harrington considered the whip. "He didn't look like someone who'd just sit there and let you do it. Matt, you got a horse?"

"Here in town? No."

"You got a Winchester?"

"Yes."

"Get it an' go down to the livery barn an' get a horse. That gunguard who spoke out at the saloon'll be down there too. The three of us'll go up where the robbery happened and sort of scout around. All right?"

Matt Wales nodded, threw a venomous

25

glare in the direction of the roadway door behind him, and walked away.

The sheriff continued on up to the rooming-house, got a light riding coat which he put on, dropped an extra box of handgun loads in a pocket, and the last thing he did before leaving was hoist his right boot onto a little bench, raise his trouser leg and put a big-bored, short-barrelled nickel-plated .41 calibre bellygun inside his boot.

At the livery barn Matt Wales and Bryce Hadley were out front with saddled animals saying nothing as they waited. When the sheriff appeared an elderly Mexican who worked as a hostler led out his horse already saddled and bridled and handed over the reins with a broad smile. He and Sheriff Harrington exchanged a wink.

They rode up through town, conscious of stares and broke over into a little lope where they had open country dead ahead. Harrington asked the whip if he could recall anything at all that he had not already mentioned, and the other man about fifteen or so years older than the lawman, shook his head. "Nothing." He cocked an eye. "There'd ought to be plenty of time though," he added, and lapsed into a dour silence until they were nearing the swale and slackened down to a steady walk as he pointed toward the west side of the road where underbrush, in places nearly as tall as a mounted man, grew in spotty profusion. "He called from over there somewhere."

But Sheriff Harrington was in no hurry. First, he rode down into the swale, studied skid marks, boot-tracks and tyre scars, then went over where the boulders had been rolled and sat there for a while before raising his eyes to the gunman's face. Bryce Hadley blew out a long breath before speaking.

"You figured right at the saloon, Sheriff. One man couldn't have rolled them big rocks into the road."

They pushed past and dismounted, left their animals behind and without haste began quartering in and out among the stands of underbush until Bryce Hadley raised a hand then pointed to a place marred by restless shod horses. Not one of them commented. The evidence was clear, not just from stamping and fidgeting shod hoof marks but also from the amount of droppings. Horses, the pale-eyed man said, had been tied back here for maybe two hours. Maybe longer.

Matt Wales sank to one knee, reading sign, and spoke without arising. "Four horses, four riders." He glanced up at Bruce Harrington as though for verification and the lawman nodded soberly as he looked elsewhere.

There were boot tracks too. The raiders had spread out after pushing boulders into the roadway. Two of them had killed time by smoking. Several brown-paper cigarette butts had been trampled underfoot.

Sheriff Harrington selected one set of tracks, traced their progress and halted close to a flourishing big thorn-pin bush. He was fairly close to the road when he leaned to very carefully part branches and peer through. This place, he was sure without mentioning it, was where the man must have stood when he hailed the stagecoach.

Bryce Hadley walked over, ignored the sheriff to gaze at the ground and to finally twist and look back where there were open places, all small, some very small, between other bushes. "What's west of here?" he asked, and got a short answer. The same as you see right here for maybe fifty, seventy-five miles. Then there's a Mex village called Ciudad Santiago."

Hadley turned back nodding at Bruce Harrington. "City of Saint George," he said, and got odd looks from his companions. Not that understanding Spanish was unusual on the South Desert. It wasn't; even people who had not been born speaking it had, if they stayed down there very long, and even if they did not want to, picked up the language which was used almost as commonly as was English. At the looks he got Bryce Hadley's little soft smile appeared. "True, I never been down here before, but I spent some time in El Paso a few years back. You either learn it over there or you starve." Having got that out of the way the gunman also said, "Gents, there's sign of four horses back yonder, and sign they rode west when they left here — now, gents, no four horses I ever saw could travel maybe seventy miles packin' riders an' all that heavy metal. Even if it was silver, the horses would give out before they went any seventy miles, with men on their backs too, but if it was gold . . . That stuffs heavy as hell and there was a lot of it — or there wouldn't have been three crates."

Matt Wales nodded grimly about the weight of the bullion boxes. "They was heavy," he averred. "Took two of us to pack each crate from the coach to the side of the road."

Sheriff Harrington was studying Bryce Hadley, whose noticeable emphasis when he'd said, 'heavy as hell' had sounded to the lawman like the remark of someone who had wrestled laden bullion boxes.

Hadley eyed Harrington. "We got a couple of hours left. Sure as hell they changed course somewhere out there. Maybe toward Camargo."

They picked up the tracks going west and followed them without haste. Once, Matt Wales worried aloud about the outlaws watching their back trail, which they might be doing, but from a considerable distance ahead, in any case Sheriff Harrington was not especially worried. He halted where the tracks abruptly turned southward. Matt looked askance at the gunman but Sheriff Harrington neither looked around nor halted long as they reined out in this fresh direction. His mind was busy. If the outlaws had indeed gone down to Camargo, then it was entirely possible they could have come from there, and had returned to cache their loot there.

Dusk arrived inexorably when they

were still several miles north of town. As Matt Wales said with resignation, "Well, we can pick it up again in the morning."

Sheriff Harrington turned due east to the stageroad. Tomorrow they would be able to locate the exact place where they'd stopped tracking.

On their way to town there was not much said. Harrington was sorting through acquaintances in the Camargo area whose reputations did not put them above suspicion, but what intrigued him most was how anyone down in Camargo had known in advance when three stages, one carrying an army payroll, would be leaving Raton, which was a considerable distant northward, up close to the Colorado-New Mexico border.

Presumably the exact departure of the coaches had been kept secret, but of course, as Harrington well knew, secrets were kept only as long as carelessness or deliberate reasons for them not to be kept, obtained, and in this instance the reasons for the secret not to be kept seemed less important than the reason *why* it was not kept.

As they were making their way down the gloomy alley on the west side of town, Sheriff Harrington asked Bryce Hadley about the other gunmen who'd come south. Hadley knew them all, not very well though adequately, but as to whether any of them would be tempted to reveal the secret of the bullion boxes, or even perhaps have acquaintances waiting in the underbush west of the swale, he had no idea.

Matt Wales made a dry remark. "Sheriff, looks to me like someone sure as hell knew. Didn't seem reasonable to me when I was settin' up there after they stopped the coach, that they just happened to pick my rig. Why not one of the other coaches, why this particular day — hell stages make that same run every blessed day an' there hasn't been one stopped down here since I been driving for the company." Matt paused, leaned to look around Hadley in the sheriffs direction, and also said, "I'll tell you how it looks to me: Someone damned well knew, an' since no one down here knew until the rigs pulled into the corralyard, why then it was a conspiracy most likely worked out up north."

Bryce Hadley, who had been listening carefully, interjected a thought. "I can tell you one thing, gents. After we left Raton we passed over some of the most desolate, gawd-forsaken, uninhabited country I ever seen in my life. Any one of those arroyos we passed through, or the rock piles beside the road would have been as good as the place they rolled the rocks into the road. Why so far south when it could have been done a hunnert miles north a lot easier?"

Sheriff Harrington was looking at the pale-eyed man when he replied. "My guess is for the same reason they left tracks heading west, then turned toward town. Because they maybe came from Camargo, or at least got a real good reason — like caching the loot — for coming down here."

When they reached the livery barn, dusk was darkening toward night. The liveryman had two feebly glowing lamps suspended from wires at appropriate intervals in his runway. He came out to take their horses and although he was clearly being consumed by curiosity, he said nothing.

They trooped up to the café, ate like horses, then trooped over to the jailhouse where Bruce Harrington lighted a hanging lamp and sank down at his desk as Matt Wales said he'd show up around sunup in the morning and departed. Bryce Hadley got comfortable in a chair beside the roadway door and said, "You're pretty close to the border, aren't you?"

Bruce understood the implication. It was not the first time he'd heard it. But this was different. "Close," he admitted.

"Suppose when we pick up the sign again in the morning it goes down over the line into Messico?"

Harrington considered the backs of his hands atop the old desk. "It's sure as hell a possibility, but not with a lot of money an' not if they ever escaped down there before, because there's whole towns down there that wait for outlaws from up here to get down there, then pounce on 'em, take everything right down to their boots, and more often than not shoot them."

"Maybe they don't know that," Hadley murmured, and Bruce Harrington smiled at him. "They know it. This bunch knows the countryside down here, which means they'd know about other things, too. Mister Hadley, they can't go riding around with hundreds of pounds of dead weight for long."

The younger man shot up to his feet, and smiled. "Most likely you're right," he said, and went out into the night.

Bruce Harrington cocked his feet atop the desk, clasped both hands behind his head and stared at the far wall.

After half an hour of speculation he would have bet his wages for a year that whoever they were, they had cached their bullion boxes within a radius of no more than a couple of miles of Camargo, and might — just damned well might — be home eating supper now, or having already done that, be getting ready for bed.

3

A Surprise

BRUCE HARRINGTON was shrugging into his riding coat about sun-up the following morning when Charles Brant walked in looking as forbidding as he'd looked at their previous meeting. He wasted no time on pleasantries nor did he sit down. "I'm going back today," he said, watching the lawman finish with the coat and head for the chair at his desk. "The hired guards are going back with me. Except for that young one who smiles all the time."

"Bryce Hadley?"

"Yes. That's his name. Sheriff, there's a thousand dollar reward."

Bruce nodded. He knew that.

"The company's in a hell of a fix. I expect you can appreciate that."

Bruce nodded again.

"As soon as I get where they got a telegraph I'll wire the army. They'll most likely send someone down here to investigate. Otherwise . . . anything you can do will be appreciated."

Bruce did not nod this time, he arose from the chair. "You can tell me a couple of things that might help, Mister Brant. For starters, how much money was in those boxes?"

The older man's bold gaze briefly clouded before he replied. "Six thousand dollars."

"Greenbacks?"

"Some of it, but mostly it was gold coinage."

"Another question, Mister Brant: When you get up north are you goin' to get the local law to investigate your men who knew about the shipment, because no one down here knew about it — except the men who let the first two stages pass and nailed the third one."

Charles Brant inclined his head like

a bull on the prod. "They'll be notified, Sheriff. So will anyone else who might help, but, the reason we went to all the trouble of masking what we were trying to do — get that damned money to its destination — is because we heard from a number of authorities that your country down here is full of fugitives and whatnot. My guess is that those men were planning on stopping a stage and were lucky enough — from their standpoint — to stop the right one."

Sheriff Harrington did not argue. He was satisfied this had not been an unplanned, spontaneous robbery, but he had learned in the corralyard yesterday not to dispute what the bull-necked man said. He pushed a pencil and a scrap of paper to the edge of the desk. "If you'll give me your address up north, when I come across anything I'll let you know."

As the older man was writing Matt Wales appeared in the roadway, recognised Brant from the rear and scowled. Bruce Harrington made a curt gesture for the driver to leave, and backed up the silent command with a black glare. Matt Wales left the doorway as Charles Brant was straightening up. He looked steadily at the sheriff for a moment then pushed out a ham-sized hand. As they were shaking, he said, "Never had anything like this happen since I been in charge. It'll come close to ruining us if we don't recover that money."

Sheriff Harrington released the older man's hand and showed a wintry smile. "Something you might like to know. That driver you fired yesterday is lending a hand. He's a good tracker. We worked until dark last night . . . If I was in his boots, Mister Brant, after the way you treated him I wouldn't pour water on you if your guts was on fire."

Charles Brant's colour mounted, his small eyes fastened onto the lawman. "Sheriff, you got a bad habit of not showing respect," he said, and turned toward the door, then hesitated before passing beyond and faced back around. "If he helps you find that money he'll be rehired. Good day."

Harrington wagged his head, waited a moment before locking up from outside and striking out for the livery barn. The sun was climbing, the morning was still chilly and would remain that way for another hour or two. As before, his companions were waiting out front with saddled horses when he got down there. Also, as before, the Mexican dayman appeared leading the sheriff's animal.

They mounted and followed the lawman around behind the barn and up the west-side alleyway. Where they emerged they could see the northbound morning stage stirring dust up ahead.

Bryce Hadley smiled thinly at its wake. "If Brant's on it, he'll be cussing everything in the Camargo country for all he's worth, and those fellers goin' north with him will be nodding their heads in agreement." Hadley laughed.

It was still cool when they turned off where their tracks from last night led back to the sign they had followed until darkness arrived.

Sheriff Harrington was quiet as they resumed tracking, but Matt Wales was not. He was a hundred or so yards ahead when he started to wave his arms and curse. The tracks they had counted on to lead them to four highwaymen had been obliterated where someone had choused a remuda of barefoot horses over the shod-horse tracks.

Bryce Hadley's brows shot up. "Who in hell drives horses in the dark?" he asked and did not get a reply as his companions began sashaying to find the southernmost extent of the barefoot marks.

Sheriff Harrington rode wearing a scowl. It deepened when they came to the farthest side of the barefoot horse tracks and although they quartered for half an hour, they could not find the four sets of shod-horse marks they'd followed the previous night.

Harrington stopped, rested both hands atop the saddlehorn and squinted southward. Beside him Bryce Hadley repeated his earlier question, but with obvious suspicion in his voice this time.

"Who drives loose stock in the dark, for Chrissake? Sheriff, do Messicans do things like that?"

Harrington brought his gaze back to the younger man. "No one does that unless they're stealing horses, and there was too many in this bunch to have been stolen from around town." When Matt Wales rode back and stopped, glaring, Harrington added a little more. "No sign of 'em continuing southward. That's just about got to mean they turned east or west below town . . . Or they rode into Camargo, an' if they did that . . . "

"Let's split up and look east an' west," the stage driver said, sounding angry. "I want to find those sons of bitches worse than I ever wanted to find anythin' in my life . . . Sheriff, if they spent the night in town, they either bedded down at the hotel or in the livery barn loft, or they got friends here who hid 'em."

Harrington and Hadley both nodded as they split up to continue their manhunt.

What Harrington hadn't said because it had only just occurred to him, was that Brant, the disgraced young gunguard and those other hired guards had all left town on the morning coach. One man had not left with the others. If anyone in Brant's three stages was part of the robbery conspiracy, he would most likely stay, if for no other reason than to ensure that he got his share.

The only man who had remained behind was Bryce Hadley.

They met in town an hour or so later to exchange information. It did not take long because they had found no tracks which could have belonged to the highwaymen.

Matt led his horse back down to the barn looking, and feeling, exasperated almost to the limit of endurance. Bryce

Hadley remained in front of the general store with Sheriff Harrington. He did not show the degree of demoralisation the stage driver had evinced. In fact as he leaned across the seat of his saddle he said, "This ought to make things easier. Whether they're still in Camargo or not sure as hell if they are someone hid them." Hadley was smiling.

Harrington nodded absently and struck out to lead his animal down yonder.

Later, back in his office with the coffee pot beginning to make boiling sounds, Sheriff Harrington leaned in his roadway door trying to guess who the stage-robbers had been and where, in his town, could they have been hidden.

They might not have been in town or, if they had been, they surely were not there now. He thought about getting astride a fresh horse and pushing the search. This time it might require more than three manhunters because the outlaws could be riding in any one of ten directions.

Before he did any more saddle-backing, in view of what they had discovered earlier in the day he went looking for the liveryman, found him swapping gossip with the proprietor of the general store and asked him if he'd known of a band of horses being driven west of town. The liveryman shook his head. The only loose-stock he'd heard of within the last couple of months had been made by some stockmen driving a big band southward for delivery to the army.

Harrington returned to the roadway. It did not seem possible that a drive could have been made close to town, even at night, without some people having either seen it or heard it, but everywhere he asked he got negative replies.

He then went down to Mex town, which had been his earlier intention, to also make enquiries. Ordinarily, the residents of Mex town were disinclined to help *gringo* law. Not all of them, but most of them.

What he encountered down there was totally unexpected. It was as though this was a feast day or a name day, some kind of cause for celebration or thanksgiving. People greeted him cordially, the stores were full, the cantina where someone was playing some kind of stringed instrument, was full of noisy, cheerful patrons. Harrington did not enter. He caught an old man he knew before the old man got inside, took him aside by the arm, and when they could speak without being interrupted or overheard he asked in candid bewilderment what everyone was celebrating.

The old man showed toothless gums in a wide smile, groped in his garments for a moment and produced three gold coins. "From *El Matador*," he exclaimed, and rolled his eyes as Harrington stared at the shiny coins.

"He came in the night, *jefe*, riding his black horse; he rode close to the windows and tossed gold to us." The old man wagged his head. "You don't believe, that's all right. He won't give you money, but that's all right. Only to those who know. *Jefe*, believe me, *El Matador* is alive. My grandfather saw him one time. A tall man dressed all in black riding a big black horse in the night, to help the very poor." The old man returned the coins to his pocket and waggled a finger. "My father never did. Neither have I. But you saw the proof. My father too was helped. *Jefe* . . . *El Matador* is ageless."

The old man went scuttling in the direction of the cantina and disappeared inside where the musician was now being assisted by male voices in song.

Harrington returned dumbly to his office, got a cup of hot coffee and went to sit at the desk. New gold coins. Why had the highwaymen, at least one of them, gone through Mex town throwing gold coins into the houses?

He did not have to be told it was

money from the bullion boxes and, after the initial shock, he was far less interested in the money itself than he was in the fact that someone playing Robin Hood, or, in this case, the mythical *El Matador*, had distributed gold coins from the robbery for a reason. *El Matador* might not have required a reason, he was a folk-hero, a legend, but that had not been any ghostly rider a couple of hundred years old, it had been a man of flesh and blood. It had also, almost beyond doubt, been one of the highwaymen.

Matt Wales walked in looking big-eyed. "I know where some of the loot is," he said, and the sheriff nodded at him. "So do I. In Mex town."

The driver was crestfallen. He dropped into a chair, screwed up his face and asked a question. "Did they tell you who left it?"

"Yeah. *El Matador*. Matt, there is no *El Matador*. What there is an' I'd give a lot to know is, why whoever flung that money around, did it?"

The stage driver did not answer. He was sitting slumped in the chair staring into space. "They're here sure as hell," he eventually murmured. "Right here in Camargo."

"Sure as hell they were last night," agreed the lawman. "Maybe that's it, Matt; they got everyone in Mex town so excited they could ride away unseen. One thing you can bet your boots on — no one in Mex town who saw any of them is going to say they did. *El Matador* arrives and disappears. That's the old legend. A handout of gold coins will sew up every lip in Mex town like nothing else could."

Bryce Hadley walked in, looked at the pair of seated men, went to a wall bench, sank down and softly smiled. "You heard about it too? That ghost-rider or whatever they call him in Mex town, tossing new gold coins through windows. Well, gents, I'll tell you one thing you can bet your lives on: At least one of them is a local otherwise he wouldn't know the story about that night-rider who throws money at folks nor how he appears like that and then disappears."

Sheriff Harrington threw up his hands. He had no dispute with what Hadley had said, what he did not like was how spreading that stolen money around, someone — maybe all four of the outlaws — had bought silence and perhaps even assistance where at least fifty percent of Camargo's residents lived.

The hefty man who owned the saloon walked in still wearing his apron. He crossed to the desk and gently placed a shiny new twenty dollar goldpiece in front of the sheriff. "A feller who hauls freight from north gave it to me not fifteen minutes ago. I asked him where he got it. He said he sold some ground maize to the store in Mex town and got paid with it . . . Sheriff; is it part of the stage robbery money?"

Harrington picked up the coin, examined it and put it down. "If it isn't," he replied. "I'll buy you a new hat, but how I'm goin' to prove it is . . . " He shook his head and leaned back.

"Where else could it come from? All you got to do is go down to Mex town, see if they got any more, and ask 'em where they got it," the saloonman said.

Three sets of eyes rose to the hefty man and stayed there while not a word was spoken until Harrington said, "They wouldn't tell me if I dragged them behind wild horses."

The saloon owner reflected on that briefly, then spoke again. "I got a Mex swamper. We're pretty close. I'm godfather to his kids. If he knows I think he'll tell me."

After the saloonman had departed Matt Wales rolled his eyes. "They're clever, Sheriff. They got the whole damned community runnin' around like chickens that got their heads lopped off. Hell, it's not goin' to take a lot of brains to guess where that money came from. The more time passes an the more folks like the barman get of that money — pretty soon won't anyone in Gringo town or Mex town say a word. That's clever, isn't it?"

Neither the lawman nor the pale-eyed man responded. Hadley eventually arose and stopped to look back from the doorway. "How much did they fling around? Three, four hundred dollars? That still leaves a lot, don't it?" He did not await an answer but walked out into the afternoon warmth on his way to the saloon.

Sheriff Harrington watched the pale-eyed man's progress toward the opposite side of the road and stirred only when Matt Wales also arose. Matt shrugged and also departed, but without speaking.

Bruce Harrington got more coffee from the old pot atop his little office stove and stood in the doorway holding the cup. The excitement was beginning to spread, as had been predicted. By tomorrow it was going to be exactly as Matt had prophesied; not a soul in Camargo from either end of town would tell the local lawman anything that might result in the impounding of that money.

Clever? More than that; it was something that had been thought out in advance. By whom?

He sipped hot coffee, watched people for a while, tossed the coffee out into the roadway and returned to his chair at the desk.

He gave up speculating about the money after a while and concentrated on those driven horses in the night. That was, at least, something people would not be reticent about and, despite his earlier failure to locate anyone who had even heard the horses, *someone* had to have either seen or heard them.

From the tracks there had to have been at least fifty animals in that drive. They had belonged to someone; they were driven by someone; they had been deliberately driven over those shod-horse outlaws' tracks!

He left the office with shadows forming, went up to the saloon and had barely more than cleared the spindle doors when he noticed how the noisy voices dwindled at his arrival.

A few patrons left, others ignored his presence and concentrated on their liquor, and three local ranch hands got a deck of cards from the saloonman, went to a far table and sat down to play poker.

Harrington had a beer and lingered over it watching the hefty man serve drinks with a totally expressionless face. Harrington smiled bleakly to himself. The barman had probably acquired a few more of those gold coins.

They were old friends but when the hefty man came to ask whether the sheriff wanted a refill his eyes never once left the countertop.

Harrington finished his drink and returned to the roadway. That affable Mexican who worked at the livery barn was emerging from the general store. Harrington caught up with him a dozen or so yards from the barn. They exchanged smiles as the Mexican blandly said, "Much excitement," and winked. Harrington followed him down through the barn to a small shack where he lived. The Mexican stopped outside to put his purchases on a wooden wash rack and rolled his eyes in an exaggerated way. "*El Matador*," he said, almost in a sigh, and the sheriff nodded, being careful not to show scepticism. The hostler looked around, looked back at the sheriff and spoke in a lowered tone of voice. "My brother saw him. He went outside to pee and saw him walking his horse among the *jacals*. *Jefe*, the number of men I have known who have seen *El Matador* I can count on the fingers of one hand." The twinkling eyes rolled again. "*Fantasma, jefe*."

"What did your brother see?" the lawman asked. "A big man on a black horse dressed all in black?"

"No, *jefe*, a tall man, *si*, but on a

bay horse. He was dressed like everyone else."

"Did he recognise him?"

"No. But he said it was dark. The man rode past within fifteen feet of him but was looking the other way. Neither of them saw the face of the other one . . . But . . . he was jingling coins in his right hand. My brother watched him approach the window of Alba Espinosa and lean from the saddle as he tossed the coins in through the window. He rode along. My brother was afraid. I asked if he'd followed the rider. He said he was shaking in his trousers. He went back to bed." The Mexican smiled slyly. "*El Matador* did not throw any money to him."

Harrington was frowning at the ground when the Mexican cut into his thoughts. "If he had been in black riding a black horse . . . " The Mexican shrugged. "I've heard that story since I was very small. So has my brother. When he told me it was a tall man dressed like a gringo cowboy on a stocky bay horse. It could not have been our hero, could it?"

Sheriff Harrington went back out front to the main roadway through Camargo and let dusk settle around him. Who else had seen *El Matador* on a bay horse without his black suit and ivory-gripped sixgun? Probably several people in Mex town and they would not tell him about it. Even the livery barn hostler's brother wouldn't tell the gringo lawman.

He returned through the runway and tapped on the hostler's door. When the Mexican looked out Harrington asked him if he had heard of horses being driven west from town a night or two before.

He hadn't.

Harrington asked who, close to Camargo, might have driven horses in the night and the old Mexican's teeth shone in early dusk. "Horsethieves, *jefe*, except that no one has said they've lost horses lately. At least not to me."

Harrington went back out front with an idea forming.

He stood a long while in the oncoming night turning it over in his mind. When he finally decided it might work because nothing else he could come up with would, he strolled up to the hotel and went to bed with weak, watery-looking stars casting feeble light earthward and no sign of a moon where there should have been one.

There were things he had to know and there were people who knew them. If they might have helped him before the scattering of gold coins, they would not do so now.

He yawned. He had never heard of anyone fearing *El Matador*, but that might be a consideration too. *El Matador*, a name which in English translated to 'The Killer', would probably be said to take a dim view of betrayal.

4

Hadley's Ride

TO the sheriff's enquiry about someone, perhaps four men, putting up at the hotel the night of the highway robbery, the proprietor shook his head. He hadn't, he said, had anyone put up at his establishment excepting of course that evil-tempered, bull-necked man and his associates who were in some way connected with the stage company, in weeks.

Sheriff Harrington left the rooming-house wondering about that statement. He was still not convinced that some of the men who had arrived in Camargo with Mister Brant were not involved. From long experience he knew that men who hired out as gunguards were just as likely to serve two masters. It was not at all unusual among gun-handy individuals.

And that brought him back to an early hunch: They had all left with Mister Brant, except Bryce Hadley.

He made a more thorough round of the community asking about those horses being driven in the night, and only hit pay dirt when he was about to give up.

He was at the blacksmith's shop. The proprietor, a muscular older man with thin hair, few teeth, and more age on him than most smiths had, knew nothing of horses being driven in the night some time before nor any other time. He was of the opinion that no one would attempt anything like that after dark if they were in their right mind, and Bruce Harrington agreed with him, but his helper, a tow-headed young man with bulging muscles shook his head at them both.

"Sure," he said in a casual contradiction, "It was the night that stagecoach was robbed." Both older men turned. The apprentice made a careless gesture.

"I sleep in the shack out back." He faced the blacksmith. "Remember me tellin' you I heard someone pawin' through the iron pile? I put on boots and britches and went out there. There was a Messican puttin' some steel scraps aside . . . I'll show them to you; they're still where he left them . . . He heard me I guess and ran like a scairt rabbit. I went after him but hell it was dark as the inside of a boot an' I lost him. I was walkin' back when I heard horses."

"West of town?" Harrington asked.

"Yes. Sounded like a hunnert of 'em, but it was a quiet night. I walked out front but, like I said, it was dark. I could place 'em by the sound but I never saw no horses nor whoever was driving 'em."

Harrington asked another question and hung on the answer. "Anything else? Horsemen in the road, anyone on foot maybe?"

"Nothin', Sheriff. Just them runnin' horses goin' west of town."

The smith was interested. "Whose horses?"

The apprentice looked annoyedly at his employer. "I got no idea, Mister Mahnken. Just horses. I went back to bed."

Sheriff Harrington had established the fact that there had indeed been a band of horses driven westward, the same band that had obliterated the shod-horse marks he had followed to the vicinity of Camargo, but more westerly, but he had already known this. What he really needed was someone who had either seen the horses being driven or who knew who the drovers had been.

But there seemed to be no possibility of getting those answers. He'd asked everyone he had been able to corner and had turned up only one man who had even heard the horses being driven, and he had seen neither the animals nor whoever had been driving them.

He crossed to the livery barn seeking the amiable Mexican hostler, who was not there. The liveryman explained that his sister was ill down in Agua Prieta. He had gone down there to do whatever he could for her. The liveryman had no idea when the Mexican would be back, and made a strained smile about that. "You know how they are; most of 'em don't own a watch and wouldn't remember to wind it if they did. They return when they're ready. Not before."

Harrington returned to the roadway. He'd already asked the hostler about those horses in the night anyway. It had simply been that, thus far, only the blacksmith's helper and the liveryman's hostler had been of any help.

The liveryman came loping up to catch Harrington before he walked away. "Meant to tell you last week, Sheriff: Your horse needs a new set of shoes."

Harrington nodded. "Take him over when you get a chance."

The liveryman agreed. He also said, "If you need a critter before Mahnken can get to him, I traded for a big, stout horse you could use. Damned near a spittin' image of your animal. Same colour, seal brown, same muscled-up build and quiet disposition. I'll keep him back, just in case."

Harrington thanked the liveryman and went up to his office where Bryce Hadley was stretched out in a chair with a cup of coffee in his hand. He smiled when the sheriff walked in. "I got an idea," he said. "Sure as hell they hid that loot. Suppose I was to make a ride out and around lookin' for disturbed dirt?"

Harrington did not scoff at the idea, but he held a private opinion that whoever the highwaymen were, in view of how clever they had been during and after the robbery, Hadley would find no disturbed earth even if the loot was buried. Those were very clever outlaws. He agreed that making such a hunt might be worthwhile, and as Hadley was leaving, Sheriff Harrington did as he'd done before, he watched the tall man cross Main Street and turn south.

On a hunch he returned to the livery barn, got the seal brown horse the liveryman had said looked like his own animal, and went up the back alley northward, kept riding until he was on high ground, then swung off to squat in front of the seal brown horse and settle himself for a long vigil.

Traffic into and out of town was about as it usually was, mostly buggies and light ranch wagons with a sprinkling of riders. He concentrated on the riders. They seemed to have a definite destination whether they were riding toward Camargo or away from it.

One rider, small in the distance, was east of town riding parallel to it. This one Sheriff Harrington watched for a long while.

He appeared to have no particular destination. The impression the sheriff got from watching him was that the rider was looking for something.

He was too distant to be recognisable

67

but the way he rode back and forth for an hour, then lower down, toward the south end of town where he repeated his sashaying manner of travelling, convinced the sheriff he was Bryce Hadley. What came as a mild disappointment was that Hadley really seemed to be searching for something.

The sheriff got thirsty. Behind him the docile big stud-necked seal brown horse dozed. The only movement he made during the hour's long vigil was to occasionally switch his tail or stamp a foot to dislodge annoying insects. He seemed to do these things unconsciously; his eyes were closed, his breathing unchanged and deep as though he were asleep.

The sun moved, the heat was not unbearable but thirst became increasingly bothersome as Bryce Hadley finished his search beyond town southward and rode on around to the west side of town. Harrington spat cotton and shook his head. Whatever else Hadley was, he sure as hell was thorough.

Once, Hadley halted to sit a long time looking downward. Harrington's spirits rose a notch until he recognised the area where Hadley was sitting. It was the area where all those barefoot horse tracks had ground out all other tracks.

Hadley did something; Harrington guessed he was rolling and lighting a smoke although he'd never seen Hadley use tobacco, then he moved out again, slowly, as always, looking at the ground.

The monotony was beginning to bother Harrington. It would have bothered him less if he'd had sense enough to bring a canteen.

When he was confident Hadley was not going to change his method of searching, he got to his feet, kicked the kinks out of his knees, swung up over leather and reined in the direction of the roadway. The last sighting he had of Hadley, the man was turning southward having completed one long search upcountry, and was preparing to do the same thing riding southward.

He wasn't going to find anything. As far as the sheriff was concerned all Hadley had accomplished was to probably arouse curiosity in people who might see him out there.

By the time the lawman returned the big seal brown horse to the liveryman the day was well along.

He tanked up on water at the pump behind the barn then headed for the café. He was too late for dinner and too early for supper but the caféman did not appear to mind although the sheriff's arrival forced him to take his feet off the countertop, fold the dog-eared newspaper he had been reading, and stoke up the stove.

The café was empty. The only noise, aside from that being made behind a hanging blanket where the caféman did his cooking, was made by a pair of fat blur-tailed flies trying to figure out how to get beneath the overturned fishbowl the caféman used to cover his pies.

When the meal arrived the sheriff

went to work on it without looking up, something which discouraged the gregarious caféman from striking up a conversation. He went back to his newspaper until another diner walked in. This time, when he took the order and padded behind the blanket to prepare it, the newcomer spoke to the sheriff.

"What the hell's Hadley doin' out yonder ridin' up an' down like he's sewin' seed?"

"Looking for some scuffed dirt where they might have buried the loot . . . Matt?"

"What?"

"I got an idea."

The stage driver did not look very enthusiastic. For days nothing had gone right, and Matt Wales was by nature one of those people whose life had ingrained into their dispositions no expectation that anything ever would go right. "We need one," he muttered noncommittally. "What is it?"

"Come by the jailhouse tonight, I'll

71

explain it to you."

The whip scowled at the big man beside him but was prevented from saying anything because the caféman brought his meal and hovered, as he'd done with Sheriff Harrington, until it was obvious that the stage driver was not in a talkative mood either; then he went mutteringly back to his newspaper.

It did not help Matt's mood any that Sheriff Harrington arose, poured silver atop the counter and without another word left the café.

The afternoon was warm and getting increasingly so as the sun sank; the earth, the rocks and trees, were releasing stored-up heat.

Harrington returned to the livery barn, found no-one down there and went to look at his own horse first, ostensibly to study the fresh shoeing job, then crossed to the opposite row of stalls and leaned there studying the big, gentle horse he had ridden north to the higher ground earlier. There was a very strong resemblance, which was not unusual since all horses had four legs, a head and tail, and, if they'd been eating regularly, pretty much the same build, some being taller or shorter, or wider or narrower, or short-backed or long-backed, but, given any similarity at all, looked pretty much the same, particularly if they were bay horses. There were more bay horses than any other kind. Bay horses never had a mane or tail that was not black.

Seal brown horses, if they were stud-necked were usually also short-backed. What the liveryman had said was quite true, Harrington's animal and the other seal brown horse bore a noticeable resemblance to each other.

On the way back to the jailhouse Sheriff Harrington was lost in thought. If his scheme worked, he had no idea what the consequences would be, but he firmly believed that any action was better than no action.

The stage driver was waiting with a pooched-out cheek where a cud of molasses-cured cut plug was lodged. He was about to pocket the plug when the lawman walked in and, being a man of good manners, offered the plug.

Bruce Harrington eyed it with the identical wariness he reserved for rattlesnakes and shook his head. "No thanks. Tried it a couple of times and threw up everything I'd eaten for a week."

Matt Wales shrugged and returned the plug to a pocket, waited until the lawman was seated then put a quizzical, but calm look in his direction.

Harrington leaned on the desk, clasped both hands and frowned. When he spoke he did not look at the stage driver, but the longer he talked the more the stage driver looked at him from perpetually narrowed eyes that widened steadily as he listened.

When silence settled, finally, the lawman looked up. Matt shifted his cud to the opposite cheek, let his gaze wander around the room for a moment then returned it to Sheriff Harrington.

"Well. All right. I don't see no reason why it wouldn't work — unless you run into *El Matador*. But I guess that ain't too likely. He's already done his good deed." Matt paused to shift position in the chair. "What, exactly, do you figure to accomplish?"

Harrington gave the same answer to the stage driver he'd already given himself. "I don't know."

Wales was beginning to look disgusted. "Gawddammit, Sheriff, you got some idea. You didn't figure all this out without havin' somethin' in mind."

Harrington reared back off the desk. "Matt, a feller told me his brother saw *El Matador*."

"The hell!"

"He said his brother left the house to pee and saw him ridin' along tossing money through windows, which is exactly the way legend says he distributes what he takes from the rich and gives to the poor."

Matt Wales, from generations of people whose mythology had dozens of examples of mysterious horsemen, and who had never come right out and said he believed in *El Matador* or did not believe in him, gazed in silence at the sheriff.

"Well," Harrington went on to say. "He wasn't dressed all in black and wasn't ridin' a black horse. He was dressed like a rangeman and was straddling a bay horse."

Matt shifted his cud again. It was impossible to say whether having such a splendid legend put down, or perhaps because his forefathers had also, at times at least, been practical people, he was beginning to put two and two together.

Harringon broke the silence between them. "What does that sound like to you?"

Matt sighed. "Like it wasn't *El Matador*."

Sheriff Harrington smiled. Matt was not going to let go of the romantic myth, but that was all right, he didn't have to. "You're right, it wasn't *El Matador*. But . . . he was doing what *El Matador* has always done. He tossed away that money to create a situation that would help him — and his friends — and which would also make the Messicans at least, mad at me if I go down there and say there is no *El Matador* and I got to impound that money."

Matt snorted. "You'll start a revolution if you do that."

"Maybe. Anyway, what I want is to grab a Messican or two who saw that particular *El Matador*."

"By scarin' the whey out of 'em?"

"Yes."

Matt rubbed his bristly jaw. "It ought to work, if that's what you want. But . . . if you grab 'em, how's that goin' to help us find the outlaws?"

"If one man saw him the other night — "

"Everyone didn't go outside to pee when he rode through, Sheriff."

Harrington nodded. "Everyone didn't have to be outside, Matt. Only a couple of people had to." The sheriff leaned on the desk again. "Someone, I'm hoping very hard, got a better look at *El Matador* than the feller who saw him while peeing. It might work. Sure as hell we're never going to be told anything if they think they got to give that money back."

Harrington rocked back off the desk again. Matt Wales was slowly nodding his head as he pushed his legs out and gazed at the scuffed toes of his boots. "An' that includes lots of folks up in Gringo town. Like the saloonman. The longer that money circulates, the more it's goin' to make a lot of folks lose their tongues." Matt smiled for the first time, a rather crooked little sardonic smile.

"Like you said, we got nothing else."

Harrington took this to mean assent and moved on to something else, but gently this time. "Matt; Mister Brant left town."

"I know that."

" . . . And took all his gunguards with him."

"I know that too. Including young peach-fuzz who made his first run as a gunguard that day."

"But one of those hired guns stayed."

Wales continued to gaze steadily at the lawman for a long time without shifting his stare or speaking ". . . Hadley?"

"Hadley."

Matt resumed his study of scuffed boots. "You think he stayed because he was mixed up in the robbery?"

"Well, if you had an interest in a share of the loot . . . "

Wales began to gently frown as he studied his boots. "I saw somethin' strange today," he said, without looking up. "Hadley ridin' up an' down west of town like he was lookin' for something. Couple fellers at the saloon called my attention to it."

Harrington explained about Hadley's idea of locating a cache, and the whip shrugged that off because it had been obvious what Hadley had been doing, but that was not what Matt had meant when he'd said he'd seen something strange.

"I watched him for a spell, along with the other fellers, then they went back inside and I was fixin' to when Hadley stopped for a spell."

Harrington nodded. "To roll a smoke."

Matt scowled at him. "He don't smoke. No. He dropped something. Like a little piece of paper." At the sheriffs steady gaze from widening eyes, Matt bobbed his head slightly. "But the strange thing was maybe ten, fifteen minutes after he'd commenced riding again, another horseman loped up, swung off, picked up whatever Hadley had dropped, and loped on toward the lower end of town. I guess he went up the back alley down there because I didn't see no more of him."

Harrington very slowly rocked forward, planted both thick arms atop the desk and looked steadily at the other man. "Did you know him? I mean, did you recognise him when he was coming toward town?"

Matt answered casually. "Sure."

5

A Time of Strain

"WHO was he?"

"A Messican, I don't know his name. He works at the livery barn."

Wales hung fire briefly before speaking again. "Got a little age. He's the only Mex who works down there. Grey-headed, sort of stocky, smiles a lot."

"Alba Moro, Matt," the lawman stated, and showed a sardonic smile. "He told the liveryman his sister was sick down at Agua Prieta and he had to go down there and look after her."

Wales had a little difficulty putting the loose ends together but eventually he looked straight at Sheriff Harrington and asked a question. "When did he tell the liveryman that?"

"I don't know. All I know is that

he's not down there and that's what the liveryman told me."

"What I'm gettin' at, Sheriff, is if I saw him out yonder this afternoon he sure as hell ain't down in Agua Prieta."

Harrington stood up. "Let's go talk to the liveryman."

But he wasn't down there, he was over at the café. The sheriff and whip looked in as they walked past, saw the liveryman among other diners at the counter and returned to the jailhouse, left the door open and got comfortable.

Eventually the liveryman appeared on the opposite duckboards to pause briefly while sucking on a toothpick before turning southward at a loose stroll.

They left the jailhouse, walked toward the lower end of town upon the west-side plankwalk and intercepted the liveryman as he was entering his runway. He turned with a casual smile, but the closer Harrington and the unsmiling coach driver got, the more strained his smile began to appear.

The sheriff said, "That Mex hostler of yours come back, did he?"

The liveryman shook his head. "Not yet. But he told me if his sister was real sick . . . What's wrong, gents?"

They did not tell him. Harrington asked two questions. "Is his name Alba Moro?"

"Yeah."

"How long's he dunged out for you?"

The liveryman shrugged, "Month, maybe six weeks. I lost a man a while back an' thought I could save money by doin' the work myself, but it wasn't worth what I paid out so when Moro come riding in lookin' for work, I hired him. An' he's good with livestock."

Sheriff Harrington's gaze went down the runway and out back as he said, "Mind if we look in his shack?"

"No, I guess not, only it seems to me —

"We won't disturb anything. He'll never know we was in there."

The liveryman's bewilderment finally atrophied. "Tell me what the hell this is all about, Sheriff."

Harrington smiled, gave the liveryman a slight slap on the back and started walking. The liveryman remained in place, but twisted to follow the progress of the whip and the lawman until they'd cleared his barn and crossed the alley, then he went irritably to his office and slammed the screen door. Moro was something rare in a hostler; he did not come up reeking of whiskey every couple of days. He was also reliable and knew horses.

The liveryman sank down upon his wired-together old chair. Well, every now and then he saw evidence of the Lord's displeasure and sure enough this was going to be another of those times. He'd lose about the best hostler he'd ever had.

He pondered about the Lord's subtle vengeance and wagged his head. Hell if the Lord had ever traded in horses and mules He would have known very well that it simply was not possible to be truthful. Maybe some of the time but not all of the time or a man'd never peddle an animal.

Across the alley the door was locked so they climbed through the shack's solitary window. Inside, the place smelled of horses. It was gloomy and crowded. They had no idea what they were searching for and that may have been the cause for not finding anything worthwhile, but they did get an idea about the Mexican. He was a tidy man, cooked with garlic and *jalapeños*, hoarded half-smoked stogies and had items of silver inlaid horse equipment hanging from pegs, all of it Mex-made and of excellent quality.

One thing caught and held the whip's attention. He frowned as he stood looking at a pair of Chihuahua spurs of thick steel with elaborate silver inlay. The rowels were half as large as a man's hand. He drew the sheriffs attention to them with a sour remark. "Anyone who'd use them things on a horse ought to be shot."

Harrington passingly gazed at the spurs on his way toward the window. The spurs meant nothing to him, he was too disappointed to even reply.

Outside in the alley again, Matt Wales was still looking bleak when they trudged up the alley toward the rear of the jailhouse, but this time it had nothing to do with the Chihuahua spurs. "He's gone," Wales said. "I'll bet you two dollars he don't come back. Sheriff, whatever Hadley dropped and Moro picked up, spooked the Messican."

Harrington was not convinced of that although he was about half of the same opinion about Moro never returning to Camargo. Whether or not he had a sister down in Agua Prieta, the town was within walking distance of the border.

When they got back to the office, Bryce Hadley was waiting. The sheriff greeted him affably but Matt Wales was almost totally without guile. He left, which was probably just as well because now that he had someone to suspect of complicity in an affair that had cost him his livelihood, it would show and Hadley, the sheriff knew, was not a fool.

He told Harrington that he'd been wrong; if they'd buried their loot around Camargo they had not buried it in the surrounding grasslands, and while he was explaining this it dawned on Harrington that Hadley's reason for making that elaborate search had not been to locate the cache, it had been to have a valid excuse to drop that scrap of paper. Why he could not simply have gone down to the livery barn and hand-delivered it to Moro the sheriff made no attempt to explain to himself, but Hadley at least must have thought there was a good reason not to, otherwise he wouldn't have spent half the day sashaying over the countryside.

When Harrington threw up his hands, Bryce Hadley was sympathetic.

"What the hell," he said. "No-one can expect miracles. You've done as much as anyone can do."

Harrington drily said, "Tell that to Mister Brant," and Hadley snorted. "Nobody ever could tell that old goat anything. His coat-tail could be on fire an' if someone tried to warn him, he'd bless them out to a fare-thee-well. When I get back I'll tell him you did everything a man could do."

Harrington gazed at the tall man. "You're leaving?"

"Not today, but soon. Sheriff, by now that damned money is down in Mexico hid out somewhere. It's been almost a week. Whoever stole it has by now got it out of the area." Hadley arose.

Harrington made a doubting scowl. "Messico? They'd have to be crazy to take it down there. That whole damned country down there lives off plundering *norteamericano* outlaws fleeing the law with stolen money."

Hadley stood a moment in thought

before he agreed. "Not Mexico then. Maybe west toward Taos, or maybe east toward civilisation."

Harrington tried to think of a way to mention the livery barn hostler and failed, so, as before, he watched Hadley's back all the way across the roadway and until he disappeared inside the general store.

Matt Wales reappeared, his eyes sulphurous and his mouth pulled down. Before he could speak the lawman asked him if he knew anyone down at Agua Prieta, and Matt nodded as he dropped into a chair.

"I lived down there for a couple of years before I hired on with the stage company an' moved up here. Why?"

"Maybe for no good reason, Matt, but Hadley got me to wondering. He mentioned something about maybe the outlaws had slipped over the line with their loot. Put that with Moro picking up a piece of paper maybe with something written on it, and leaving town . . ."

"You said Moro left town the day before."

"No. I said he told the liveryman he was going to leave. That was yesterday. He did leave, evidently, but not until he picked up that message Hadley dropped. Hadley mentioned the border and Messico and Moro told the liveryman he had to go down to look after a sick sister. Agua Prieta, Matt."

The stage driver sat a long time in morose silence before speaking. "I could go down there. Hell, I know everyone worth knowing in that border country."

Harrington was beginning to have the identical feeling he'd had a number of times in his life, the same feeling wolves feel when they're making a promising stalk.

"When can you go, Matt?" he asked, and the whip gave him a sardonic look. "Since I ain't workin' I can go any time . . . Tonight on the southbound."

Harrington arose. "Buy you a drink," he said, heading for the door.

They ambled up to the saloon where the overweight saloonman set up two jolt glasses with a bottle between them, and eyed his customers. "I got three, four more of them gold coins across the bar," he said. "Got 'em legal and all, Bruce."

The lawman nodded almost casually. His mind was not on *El Matador's* largesse at the moment. He waited until the barman had departed then said, "Remember that idea I told you about?"

Matt nodded dourly.

"Maybe tonight, Matt."

Wales turned slowly but said nothing as he gazed at the sheriff. He downed his whiskey and refilled the little glass, pushed the bottle toward Harrington and finally spoke. "Where are you goin' to get the money?"

"I got it.

"In gold?"

"Yes."

Wales shifted position slightly against the bar. "I got to tell you, Sheriff

— that's a crazy idea. Is this money from your savings?"

"Yes."

"Well, you'll never see it again, no matter how things turn out."

Harrington thinly smiled. "Mister Brant's reward — remember?"

Wales remembered and nodded to indicate that he did. "But the way I figure your idea, you got about one chance out of maybe thirty of ending up a winner."

Harrington did not refill his little glass. He was not by nature much of a gambler, but on the other hand he had his teeth into the matter of the stolen payroll and right now he was beginning, for the first time since the robbery, to feel hopeful.

"It's been a week now," Matt grumbled. "If they ain't got that money to hell an' gone away from here by now I'll be real surprised." After making that statement Wales slowly raised his head and scowled at the lawman. "Maybe not?"

93

Harrington did not commit himself except to say to move that much weight would require several horses, and that would be chancy, which the outlaws would know. Then he also said, "See what Moro is up to down there an' when you get back maybe I'll have stumbled onto something at this end."

They left the saloon and parted out front, the sheriff heading for his jailhouse and Matt Wales walking in the direction of the stage company's office.

Wales had the least to do before leaving town; stuff a few necessaries into an old warbag and wait. Sheriff Harrington was occupied through most of the afternoon, assembling the things he would need, and it was almost dusk before he was satisfied and was leaning in the jailhouse doorway when the southbound stage passed through town at a dead walk. Wales nodded and Harrington nodded back before turning back inside to drape his empty cup from a wall peg near the stove and stand a while in deep thought.

Dusk arrived slowly this time of year. Later, when summer was in full bore, it would amount to little more than the blink of an eye after sunset and before nightfall.

Harrington made a round of the town, stopped longest down at the livery barn where he and the liveryman chatted briefly. The liveryman asked if Harrington intended to join the meeting at the fire house after supper to help make the decision about buying new running-gear for the town's horse-drawn pumper, or maybe to use the money — in his opinion — more wisely by buying a new pumper for which the money that would be required to repair the old one would go a long way toward the purchase.

Harrington lied. "I'll be up there. Unless something comes up. Any news from your hostler yet?"

"Not a word. But they never write, any more than they ever show up when they say they will."

"I never heard him mention a sister down in Agua Prieta, did you?"

The liveryman shook his head. "No, but we never talked about personal things anyway. Sheriff; you find what you were lookin' for in his shack?"

This time Harrington did not have to lie. "Nope."

"What were you lookin' for?"

"Can't exactly say. I didn't climb in there expecting to find anything, and that's exactly what I found. Nothing."

"What made you figure you'd find something?" the liveryman asked.

Harrington glanced up the roadway where three horsemen were arriving out of the shadowy pre-night at a dead walk. He needed an excuse to end this conversation and nodded in the direction of the horsemen. "Looks like strangers up yonder. It's not Saturday night but in my job a man's got to sort of expect trouble even on week nights."

He walked away. The liveryman watched him pass the jailhouse on his way toward those three riders who were tying up out front of the saloon, then he shrugged and went back down the shadowy runway.

A man did not very often get into trouble minding his own business, and although the liveryman was very curious he'd followed a lifelong rule of not looking too deeply into the affairs of others. Basically he was one of those people to whom real trouble was anathema.

Harrington entered the saloon as the hefty owner was gingerly climbing off a chair after having fired up one of the hanging lamps. The three men relaxing against the bar had been served and beyond nodding in the direction of the badge on the large man's chest, paid no more attention to Harrington than they'd been paying to the hefty man dragging his chair around as he lighted lamps.

Harrington got a glass of beer and raised it as a shield over the rim of which to study the newcomers. They were strangers; at least he was certain he had never seen them in Camargo before. But that did not have to have any significance; this time of year ranchers were moving livestock, or sweating — and swearing — at marking grounds. Hired hands came and went.

One thing made Harrington wonder. Each of those three strangers wore their sidearms low and tied down, which did not have to mean much either. Most riders tied their holsters down as they also used cross-straps or thongs to prevent their weapons from being jolted out of their holsters when horses loped or trotted, or shied.

He moved a little closer to strike up a harmless conversation and got a surprise. The three men were not only affable, they told him they'd just arrived in town to have one drink and maybe some supper before hunting him up; they'd heard about the army payroll being stolen; they were professional manhunters. Bounty hunters.

They were youngish men. Only one had any grey and that was only a sprinkling at the temples.

Harrington leaned and visited, while in the back of his mind resentment was stirring. As an authorised lawman he did not view bounty hunters kindly. Not because he particularly objected to human vultures, but because such men got in the way, were underfoot. If they hung around long enough they became obnoxious.

They followed him down to the jailhouse where he gave them a blunt ultimatum: Stay in Camargo and he'd lock them in a cell and feed the key to a turkey. Bryce Hadley walked in. Harrington introduced the strangers by name only. When they arose to depart Hadley offered to show them where the rooming-house was. The three strangers nodded woodenly toward the sheriff and departed with Hadley, who would probably learn who the strangers were. Harrington smiled about that. Unless he was very much mistaken Hadley would want them out of the area even more than Harrington did.

Harrington had never been very good at killing time and he had not improved in that respect since he'd hunkered up yonder, backgrounded by brushy hills, nearly dying of thirst while watching Bryce Hadley sashaying all over hell ostensibly searching for a cache which, Harrington rather thought now, Hadley had known was not out there.

Twice Harrington went into his back room, used for storage and little else, and each time he returned looking if not elated, at least satisfied. He drank enough coffee to float a boat, made a short skirmish around town to let himself be seen, and stopped to look in down at the livery barn.

There was no one around. The horses had been fed. The liveryman was probably at either the café or the saloon. Harrington looked in on his horse, gave a passing glance at the other seal brown and returned to the roadway resolutely walking toward the lighted jailhouse office.

The night was still young, and that

annoyed him. Any other damned night time flew past. Tonight it went along like it was tied to a tree.

He wondered about Matt Wales down at Agua Prieta. He also thought about the livery barn hostler, Alba Moro, and was not entirely happy because the Mexican had been pleasant, obliging and friendly, and of course those would be the attributes a man would show if he had a curious lawman nosing around. Still, Harrington had liked the man.

He blew down the mantle of the office lamp and locked up from inside, which was a very simple process. He dropped an oak *tranca* into the steel hangers on each side of the door and shoved a bridge spike into the slanted hole on the lifting side. That prevented the oak bar from being raised from outside.

He went to the storage room, lighted a small lamp, closed the door between the office and the storeroom and stood a moment without moving.

101

6

Return of the Hero

MEX town was not entirely different from Gringo town, except perhaps in ways that could have been explained by economics. There were few lamps down there, more candles which could be made in abundance very cheaply, areas for monetary amusement were fewer, consisting mainly of one large cantina where men gathered to drink, lie and gossip about as they did in Gringo town, and for women there were small gatherings in various residences, and in the massive thick-walled mission, old beyond reckoning and at present reduced to the status of a local church with only an occasional itinerant priest. Women with covered heads could be found there almost any time of day, and late into the nights. It was a hard life, praying did not make it noticeably better, but that did not prevent the women of Mex town from kneeling with their rosaries praying very sincerely that it would get better.

It never did.

There were bands of mixed sheep and goats, maize patches, vegetable gardens. As many people worked out as could, but money had always been hard to get and harder to keep.

Mex town was an insular place. There were no such things as secrets. There was no overt friction between the two parts of Camargo, but inevitably, since the people were so different, their day to day relationship was based on one's ability to pay for labour, the other's ability to provide it.

A source of scoffing for years was the almost childlike faith of Mexicans. The superstitions, legends and myths were not so much ridiculed in Gringo town as they were ignored.

But Mexicans born north of the

border were not Quetzlcoatl people. They had their fantasies but not on the scale of Mexicans born in Mexico.

It may even have been that they would not have believed all those things if, being very poor, they had not required something to admire because their own daily lives were founded upon an inherent hopelessness.

It could also be assumed that at least some of them did not believe in the myths, the legends, the promises which had never been kept, but these, like the dry scepticism of Alba Moro, seemed to teeter upon a wish to believe, and a practical sense of doubt. In any case doubters were few and it only took some small marvel to rekindle their — at least temporary — beliefs.

There is always a 'Robin Hood,' an *El Matador*, and perhaps at one time such individuals did exist, but that was not the real issue. Poverty, degrees of hopelessness were the issues, and inevitably they spawned The Hero. He lived in the heart. He appeared and re-appeared. Every generation knew him, he was the physical embodiment of the heart's need.

That he could appear twice in the same week was not questioned. Unusual, yes, but so very welcome when he appeared on a powerful black horse — actually seal brown but at night a seal brown horse appeared as black — attired in black with a glimpse of an ivory-handled Colt in a black holster, walking his horse without haste as *fantasma* would do because he feared nothing, and nothing physical could harm him.

He entered Mex town from the east, which had its significance to the devout. He came slowly and deliberately passing among the mud houses and faggot corrals. Dogs barked, people who were uneasy about dark nights listened but rarely peeked out.

He did not ride a straight course, he zig-zagged on a loose rein, occasionally leaning as he passed to pitch a gold coin or two through a shutter-less window. He did not hurry. In fact when he had passed from east to west he reined around and repeated his ride from south to north.

Lights went out, people became still. They heard the unmistakable sounds of a slow-pacing horse. Some people old enough to go outside were prevented from doing so by those who warned against it.

As *El Matador* was passing along an old man crept forth, eyes alight. A barren wife stood in a doorway. A burly, unshaven man opened his door very quietly and stood in the darkness without going outside. He was honestly puzzled.

The tall man on the black horse briefly nodded to some, seemingly missing few. His hatbrim was far enough forward to cast his features in darkness. It was said afterwards that although his smile was faint and his eyes gleamed in the darkness, he seemed benign.

The interlude lasted less than half an

hour, then *El Matador* disappeared, not difficult on a moonless night dressed all in black riding a dark horse, and the legend was perpetuated.

Mex town was as silent as a tomb for the rest of the night. Gringo town, with no knowledge that the legendary horseman had again appeared, knew nothing until inhabitants of Mex town who were employed in Gringo town showed up for work the following morning, very impressed, big-eyed with wonder — and with gold coins.

Bryce Hadley appeared at the jail-house shortly after breakfast looking baffled. He told the sheriff it was being said along the gossip circuit that the damned spook the beaners called *El Matador* had appeared last night in Mex town tossing gold coins around.

Harrington smiled indulgently. "When you've lived down here as long as I have, you shrug off a lot of that kind of talk. It's their nature to believe all sorts of silly stuff."

Hadley frowned at the sheriff. "All right, but if a lot of people see something . . ."

Sheriff Harrington went to the front window and stood looking out. "It's a local legend. People have been seeing *El Matador* for a hundred years. Maybe longer." He turned. "No one lives that long. It's a myth."

Hadley looked around. "The gold coins are a myth? Hell Sheriff, they are real. Folks have seen them this morning."

Sheriff Harrington turned to gaze dispassionately at the other man for a long while in silence, then returned to his desk and sat down.

"All right. The gold money is real. Why would someone who sure as hell isn't a ghost, throw gold coins around down in Mex town? I'll make a guess: To make a diversion of some kind. I can't figure any other reason. It worked too, didn't it? The whole blessed community, not just down in Mex town, isn't talking about anything else."

Bryce Hadley sat staring at the lawman. "What . . . A diversion? For what? That don't make any sense, Sheriff."

Harrington smiled. "I told you it was a guess. Maybe you can come up with something better."

Hadley slowly shook his head and arose. "I sure can't," he said as he moved to the doorway.

Bruce Harrington did as he'd previously done, he watched Hadley cross the road, but this time he too left the jailhouse and until he got down to Mex town he did not stop. He was thoroughly familiar with the area and without hesitation he approached a particular *jacal* where an old man was out back in a little faggot corral where the smell of goats and sheep was almost overpowering. The old man turned when he had finished making his morning count, saw the sheriff leaning there and was momentarily startled. Then he smiled.

"*Buenas dias*," he murmured and the sheriff replied in the same language, then switched to English. "Arturo, were you among the lucky ones last night?"

The old man laughed. "Last week, not last night. *Jefe*, too much good fortune can ruin people."

"Did you see him?"

"*El Matador*? Yes. From my doorway." The old shepherd came closer as he gestured. "Big, all in black riding his black horse." Arturo dropped both arms to his sides and peered from beneath thick, nearly white eyebrows. "I could have walked out and touched him."

"Why didn't you?"

The old man was aghast. "Why should I?" he countered. "*Jefe*, do you know how I have lived so long? Because I'm a prudent man. Besides, why should I want to touch him?"

"Who else saw him?"

"My son-in-law, the *arriero*." The old man batted at a nibbling goat. "Do you know him?"

"Yes. Patricio Castillo. Did others see him?"

Arturo tugged at the hem of his ancient coat and the goat tugged back. "Others? I don't know . . . get away you, before I give you a kick." The goat did not let go, Arturo kicked it and it not only let go, it walked away.

The sheriff retraced his steps until he reached a larger mud-walled cube where there were several corrals, much larger, for horses and Mexican mules. The mules were small, at the most eight hundred pounds, but they had a deserved reputation on the south desert for unbelievable strength and endurance. They also had a reputation for treachery, but that was not exclusive to Mexican mules.

A buxom woman was out back doing laundry in a dented big old pan. Her husband, a burly, powerful looking quite dark man was idling in the doorway watching. When Sheriff Harrington appeared around a corner the big Mexican eyed him, nodded,

nodded toward his wife's swaying hips and rolled his eyes. Then he laughed and Harrington laughed with him which brought the sturdy woman around staring.

The *arriero* took Harrington inside and offered him red wine at a scarred table. His very dark eyes settled on his guest's face and in almost accentless English he said, "*El Matador*, eh? Well; I saw him. I stood outside and looked straight at him and he looked straight back." The powerful shoulders rose and fell, "He didn't open his mouth and neither did I. You don't like the wine?"

Harrington quickly hoisted the glass. It was very mellow wine. He put the glass aside. He and Patricio Castillo had been friends off and on for years. Harrington said, "Arturo told me you saw him."

The big man sat opposite the sheriff and nodded without speaking.

"Patricio . . . Last week he was here too."

Another nod from the big man, but this time with a hint of a flicker to his gaze.

"You saw him that time too?"

"Yes. I was out back feeding the mules. I don't think he saw me because the faggots of the corral are taller where he passed by. Close enough for me to almost have touched him, Sheriff."

"Kind of late at night to be feeding, wasn't it. About midnight?"

Patricio Castillo shrugged. "Late, maybe. I had only come in with the pack mules a short while before. I had to care for them." The *arriero* leaned on the table. "I watched him throw some coins through the bedroom window of Alba Espinosa. There were candles in the bedroom that shone through the window." The Mexican paused to half empty a glass of wine. He made a sly smile afterwards. "It was a bay horse, Sheriff, not a black one. There was no ivory grips on his Colt. He was tall, yes, but he was dressed as you or I might be." Castillo saw the intent expression on the sheriff's face and broadly smiled. He was enjoying this moment.

"If you saw all that, Patricio, what else did you see — his face?"

"*Si.*"

Harrington stared hard. "You saw his face?"

"I just told you that. Yes, I saw his face."

"Did he see you?"

"I don't think so. As he was reining away from the window he looked southward and rode along."

"Patricio — "

Castillo held up a work roughened large hand, and smiled even more broadly. "Sheriff, do you know how hard it is to compete with freighters and even the stage company which also hauls light freight? A mule-train is slow, it can't begin to pack the supplies they put into wagons and coaches. It is very hard work, and mules, like my horses, eat their heads off. I go all the way down to — "

"Hold it," Harrington exclaimed,

holding up a hand. "You damned robber."

The big Mexican was not insulted, nor did his grin diminish, but his very dark eyes were fixed on Sheriff Harrington in an intractable way. "Sheriff, I barely made it last week and this time he rode past my house. Others got gold coins. I have to leave again in a couple of days, go all the way down to Mexico, pick up whatever I can down there and come all the way back up here."

Sheriff Harrington leaned back, rummaged in a trouser pocket, pushed a closed fist to the middle of the table and opened it. Five gold coins fell atop the table.

Patricio Castillo looked, started to speak, looked at the coins again and leaned back gazing inscrutably at the lawman. After a while he said, "You?"

"All I'll tell you is that I want you to identify that man for me."

But Castillo continued to stare hard

115

across the table. "That was you last night?"

"Who is he, Patricio?"

"I don't know his name. I've seen him around town a few times."

"When was the last time you saw him?"

Patricio had made his decision about the other question and picked up the coins to examine each before pocketing it. "The day I left with the mules to go down to Agua Prieta for a pack load, he was riding east of town, back and forth up and down."

Silence settled between them broken only by the watery sounds of the buxom woman out back at the tub. When Sheriff Harrington finally arose he said, "You've just been paid to go stand near the livery barn. When I walk past with another man all you have to do is nod your head if he's the same one you saw last week outside your corral. If it's not the same man you shake your head. That's all."

Patricio Castillo arose. "Those are

good wages for standing in the shade, no?"

"And Patricio — not a word. Not even to your wife."

The black eyes widened. "You're not a married man or you wouldn't have said that. Least of all to my wife, otherwise, she would know I have money."

Sheriff Harrington returned to Gringo town and watched the roadway from his front door. He did not see Bryce Hadley among the pedestrians so he strolled across to the general store. He was not there either. Harrington went up to the saloon. There were only three ragged old men playing matchstick poker close to the stove.

He returned to the roadway with a mildly uneasy feeling. He could not imagine what might have spooked Hadley; he had to be somewhere around town. If something had spooked him Harrington was going to have to start out all over again, and this time with no idea where to start.

He walked southward past the gun-smith's shop, the abstract office, past the barber's shop — and stopped, turned back and looked through the window a second time. The barber waved with a razor in his hand.

He was shaving Bryce Hadley.

Harrington went down a few doors and leaned quietly to wait. He saw the large Mexican packer walk north of the livery barn, find a shady place and take up an unobtrusive position down there.

When Hadley eventually emerged from the tonsorial parlour and saw the sheriff loafing nearby, he approached him while using a blue bandanna handkerchief to dislodge hair that had got beneath his collar.

Harrington wrinkled his nose. Hadley chuckled. Neither of them commented on the elegant scent of jasmine Hadley exuded. Harrington jerked his head. "Walk down to the barn with me."

Hadley did not object but he asked about the reason and the sheriff smiled wintrily at him. "Something I'd like to ask your opinion about."

They crossed the road and encountered the liveryman walking northward. He stopped, nodded to them and said, "Sheriff, I can make you a hell of a price on that seal brown horse."

Harrington smiled. "I was just going to show him to Mister Hadley. See what he thinks of him."

The liveryman was immediately interested. "I'll go with you," he said, and Harrington shook his head. "No. Just the two of us, if you don't mind."

The liveryman turned to watch them walk southward, rolled his eyes because no one seemed to trust him even when he was being perfectly honest, and resumed his hike up to the leather shop where he'd left torn harness to be repaired.

There was enough heat in the day to encourage an interest in shade. A number of old men were on benches toward the lower end of town, in position for their daily vigil for the incoming northbound stage coach. Not often, but just often enough there would be a woman passenger. When there was the old men watched, scarcely breathing as they alighted. Sometimes the glimpse of a female ankle did more for their drying juices than a big jolt of the hefty barman's popskull.

There was also a large, muscular Mexican leaning in shade as Harrington and Hadley strolled past. He seemed to be busy with a callous on one palm and they ignored him until they came abreast, then the big lawman turned his head, the burly Mexican stopped picking the callous, looked Harrington straight in the eye and very gently inclined his head.

When they finally reached the barn and turned down the cool, shadowed runway Bryce Hadley said, "If you want advice about a horse, Sheriff, you could do a lot better'n me."

They stopped in front of the stall of the seal brown gelding Harrington had used while his own horse was over at the blacksmith's shop. Hadley leaned to look in. "Looks stout enough," he said. "Acts gentle." He stepped back. "About the only thing I know about horses is that if they're not sound they'll give out when you're riding them . . . Sheriff; what in the hell are you doing with that sixgun?"

Harrington did not reply. He stepped back and gestured with the gun toward the back alley. When they got back there he said, "North. Up to the back of the jailhouse."

Hadley obeyed even as he protested. Where he stopped behind the jail Sheriff Harrington shoved his sixgun into the tall man's soft parts, cocked it, then emptied Hadley's holster, stepped back and jerked his head. "Inside. It's not locked."

Hadley paused on the top step and would have turned but a gunbarrel being jammed into his back over the kidneys made him wince, push open the door and walk inside.

7

'Tomorrow, Sheriff.'

UP to this point Sheriff Harrington had acted according to a lawman's custom, but from this point on he was less confident. He wordlessly fiddled with the little iron stove and shook the coffee pot. There was brew in it but not enough so he methodically went about putting another fistful in and tipping in more water. But he did not fire up the stove, he went to his desk sat down and eyed his captive.

Hadley, who had watched every move, sat on a wall bench staring back. If he was upset it did not show, but Harrington knew that much about the gunguard: Nothing ever appeared to upset him. Finally, Hadley asked a question.

"You got a reason, Sheriff?"

"More than one," replied the lawman, leaning both arms atop the desk. "Where is it?"

"Where is what?"

"The money. Wait a minute. Before you start lying, I'll tell you something. It was no accident that you hung back when everyone else went up north with Mister Brant."

"I told you, I liked the country an' I wanted to see how that mess would end."

"I'll bet you did," the sheriff stated drily. "Now answer a couple of questions for me. First, why didn't you just walk down to the livery barn and tell the hostler what you went through all that elaborate horsebacking to tell him in the note? Second, who drove those horses west from town to wipe out your tracks?"

Bryce Hadley sat a moment regarding the big man before finally shaking his head. "You think I had a hand in that payroll robbery? You're crazy. Why would I hang around Camargo if I'd been tangled up in that?"

"Lots of reasons, Hadley. Why would you ride through Mex town pitching gold coins through windows? Why would you ride all over hell looking for a buried cache you knew you wouldn't find? Why would you drop a note for Moro to find? How did you know Moro would find it? How did you know someone would blot out your tracks with that band of unshod horses?"

Hadley laughed. "Is that all you got?" he asked in derision, and leaned forward looking steadily at Harrington. "You better have somethin' better than questions to hold me, Sheriff."

This time it was Harrington's turn to show humour, but he didn't laugh, he coldly smiled. "I can hold you until the cows come home," he said quietly, gazing steadily back. "You don't know how south desert law works, do you? I can hold you until you're grey-headed."

"On what charge?"

"Suspicion."

Hadley snorted. "Suspicion? That's all?"

"I just told you — you don't know south desert law. We got reason to operate different than they do up in the states. Territories are administered by the military. It's not like the states that got civil law. Territories even have military governors." Harrington leaned back. "You know how far the nearest military administrative command is from Camargo? Four days ride. There's somethin' else that might interest you: Right now they got a revolution goin' on down in Mexico. That keeps the soldiers busy as a kitten in a box of shavings. Even if I sent word that I got someone in custody who knows about that payroll robbery, it'd take four days for my messenger to get over there, four days for him to get back — an' even if they wanted to spare the men to ride back with the messenger, which I'd lay you fifty to one they don't, I can tell you from experience nine times out of ten they show up late, if they show up at all . . . Now then, that's why I can hold you. On suspicion of robbing an army payroll until the army gets the time to come up here. Want a guess? Two months. Maybe six months. Want to know something else, Mister Hadley? Before that much time goes by I'll know the whole blessed story, an' when I do I'll shackle you in irons, take you to a military guardhouse and leave you there — and you'll likely rot in one of those little cells because the army don't hold trials any oftener than they got to — and — they'll find you guilty. They always find fellers like you guilty."

Throughout the sheriffs harangue Bryce Hadley sat gazing across at him. When the lecture was finished he eased back against the wall with nothing to say until the sheriff stood up, took down his ring of keys and jerked his head for Hadley to precede him into the gloomy, poorly lighted cell room.

As Harrington was locking him in Bryce Hadley said, "You think that robbery was done by one man?"

Harrington straightened up from locking the door as he replied: "No. One man was all the fellers on the stagecoach heard, but there had to be someone down here ready to chouse those horses over your tracks, an' there's the livery barn hostler. I'd guess it was a pretty well organised effort by several men . . . And just to make it easier for you to sleep tonight I'll tell you something else: The driver of that stage you stopped is down in Agua Prieta spying on Alba Moro. I could tell you more but I'm not going to."

Harrington returned to his office, slammed the intervening door, locked it and returned to his desk. With a man like the one he'd just locked up it was difficult to guess what his reaction would be, until he'd had at least the rest of today and until tomorrow morning to assess his position. One thing Harrington thought Hadley believed now, and it was the gospel truth whether he believed it or not, Harrington could indeed hold him as long as he wanted to.

The liveryman walked in looking quizzical. "That friend of yours like the horse?" he asked, and took the chair beside the door, softly scowled and said something else. "You know old Dave Stern who ranches southwest of town a few miles? He come into the barn a while back lookin' for Alba Moro."

"Why?" asked Sheriff Harrington.

"He didn't say. When I told him Alba'd gone down south to look after a sick relative the old man got red in the face and went stamping out of the barn." The liveryman returned to his original topic. "Tell you what, Sheriff: I'll make you one hell of a price on that seal brown horse."

"How much?"

"Well, seein' it's you an' all, an' you'll use him in your work protectin' the town — "

"How damned much!"

"Sixty dollars." At the glare he got the liveryman barely paused to draw breath as he continued speaking. "He's gentle as a lamb, sound as new money, stout as a bull and gentle. He's an all-around good saddle animal. That kind of a horse — oh yeah, I almost forgot — he's a combination horse too, saddle him or hitch him to a buggy. That kind of an animal — "

"Thirty dollars," the lawman growled and the liveryman's eyebrows shot up. "Thirty dollars, for Chrissake. Sheriff, you know that horse. You can't fault him. I buy an' sell 'em by the dozens every year an' that seal brown's the best — "

"Thirty dollars! I don't need another horse."

"Like hell you don't. When you rode out last night if you'd owned him you could have spared your regular horse — "

"Who said I rode out last night?" the sheriff snarled.

129

The liveryman sat big-eyed regarding the law officer. "Hell, I didn't know it was a secret . . . I was comin' in the front when you rode out the back an' turned south toward Mex town."

"Me?"

"Yes, you. I saw . . . " The liveryman suddenly stopped speaking, his already wide-open eyes staring. "Gawddamn," he almost whispered. "I wondered. I never seen you dressed like that before." The liveryman fidgeted but did not take his eyes off the sheriff's face. "Last night in Mex town that ghost-rider they believe in rode through. *El Matador*." The liveryman stopped speaking but it was clear from his expression that he was drawing a shocking conclusion.

Bruce Harrington leaned forward on the desk. "You're crazy. Were you up at the saloon? Maybe you saw someone ride a horse out, but if he wasn't dressed like me — "

"He was riding your horse, Sheriff."

Harrington threw up his hands and

glared as he resumed his leaning-forward position. "You spread this crazy story around town — "

"You got my word, I won't mention it to a soul." The liveryman stood up. "If you want to give folks money, specially them folks down there that don't have any, I think it's a real fine thing." The liveryman got to the door before turning and dropping Harrington a conspiratorial wink. "Nobody'll ever know from me. If that's the way you want it, take my word for it, that's the way it's goin' to be."

Harrington blew out a fierce curse after the liveryman had departed, arose to stand by the barred front wall window looking out as he speculated about this development. People gossiped, particularly if they had something as juicy as this to gossip about. He had known the liveryman a long time. To his knowledge the man was not a gossip, but he'd probably never had anything as electrifying to gossip about. For a damned fact what he had figured out was worth at least five free drinks up at the hefty man's saloon.

Of course, a lot of folks wouldn't believe him. Maybe most folks wouldn't. It would certainly be incongruous and out of character for a lawman most of them had known since he'd arrived in the Camargo country.

Harrington crossed to the café for a pail of coffee and another one of hash for his prisoner. On the way back he saw the liveryman and old Fred Mahnken standing in front of the blacksmith's shop talking. As he was re-entering the jailhouse he thought bleakly that if the liveryman told the blacksmith that story he'd be derisively laughed at. Old Mahnken wouldn't believe that yarn any more than he'd believe in the Second Coming complete with golden trumpets and golden chariots unless he saw it himself.

Bryce Hadley was sitting on his bunk when the sheriff growled for him to stay there as he unlocked the door placed the little pails on the floor and relocked the door from the outside.

Hadley ignored the food and seemed to be considering the man who had brought it. Maybe Harrington had been wrong; maybe the gunguard did not require as much time to think about his predicament as Harrington had thought he might.

As Harrington was turning away the prisoner arose and called him by name. "Sheriff Harrington."

The lawman turned back, expressionless and silent.

"Suppose we talked sort of rational about this. Maybe you can keep me locked up like you said, but all that's goin' to do is waste a lot of time for both of us."

Harrington's recent encounter with the liveryman had not improved his mood. He said, "All I want to hear from you is where that money is."

Hadley went to the front of the cell and held to the steel straps with both hands. "I know just one thing for a fact that happened the night of that robbery."

Harrington continued to stand in the middle of the little corridor, scowling and silent.

"Moro got some old raggedy-pantsed horse rancher named Stern to bring up a *remuda* of horses."

"How did he manage that?" Harrington asked.

"He figured to maybe buy horses, trail them down into Messico and sell them."

Harrington snorted. "You really don't know this country, do you? There's not a man alive who could trail horses down over the line by himself and not have them taken away from him, an' maybe get himself killed in the bargain. Ten men would have trouble doing that, even if they were armed to the teeth. Hadley you got to do better."

"He did arrange for that horse-rancher to bring up a *remuda*. He helped the rancher corral them out behind the livery barn."

134

Harrington strolled back closer to the cell. "An' he just happened to bust them out westerly after he heard you other fellers coming down here, is that it?"

"I told you — all I know is that Moro arranged for the rancher to bring in a band of horses for him to look at."

Harrington looked steadily through the steel straps for a moment, then turned on his heel and went back up front, loudly barred the door and went to the *olla* for a drink of cold water.

As he was drying his chin he smiled. That was a start. Hadley hadn't needed all night to decide he was in a predicament that required resourcefulness to get out of, and he had just revealed that he knew Alba Moro very well.

Harrington went over to the café for supper. When the caféman, whose eyes were round with consuming curiosity, asked who his prisoner was, the sheriff looked at him with a wolfish smile and did not answer.

Later, up at the saloon after making a round of the town, Harrington had a glass of tepid beer and enjoyed it slowly as he thought that he just might damned well be getting close to something. Until the barman came along to say, "There's talk. Folks are grumblin' about you not ridin' out with a posse."

Harrington's mild elation evaporated as he gazed at the hefty man. "What would I be riding out with a posse to find?"

The hefty man changed the subject rather quickly. "Did you know *El Matador* returned to Mex town last night?"

"The hell."

"For a fact. That Mex who cleans up for me said he saw him plain as day."

"Did he? Ridin' his black horse and all?"

The hefty man did not like the sound

136

of the sheriffs voice and reddened. "All I know is what he told me. An' he showed me a couple of gold coins." When Harrington sipped beer and did not immediately respond the hefty man leaned down and lowered his voice. "It was him sure as hell, Sheriff. Others also saw him. Y'know, this swamper of mine is a practical feller with a wife an' kids. I've let him mind the bar a few times. Mostly to see if he'd help himself to the money drawer. He never did."

Harrington pushed the empty glass away. "*El Matador*," he said musingly, a hard twinkle to his gaze. "He's got to be at least a hundred and fifty years old."

"Well," the hefty man said and avoided the lawman's eyes as he made a big sweep of the bartop with a moist rag.

"Do you know old Dave Stern?" the lawman asked.

The hefty man stopped mopping. He looked relieved they were off the *El*

Matador topic. "Sure." He pointed with his empty hand. "Over there behind the stove with another old stockman."

As the sheriff walked in the direction of the massive old cast iron cannon heater the hefty man leaned atop his bar and watched Harrington's progress with troubled eyes. No one in their right mind believed in ghosts — until they saw one. He hadn't actually seen one but he had a first hand account of one from someone he trusted absolutely and that was as convincing as a man could get without seeing the ghost himself.

When Sheriff Harrington appeared at the table, which was partly in shadows because of the intervening big iron stove both the weathered, lined and faded older men sitting with a bottle between them looked up. They nodded, but it took a moment for them to do it.

Harrington pulled out a chair, dropped down and smiled at Dave Stern. "Haven't seen you in town for a coon's age," he said, and the older of the two old gaffers fixed the lawman with a gimlet glare.

"Wouldn't be here now if a Messican hadn't talked me into bringin' up some horses he wanted to buy."

"Did he tell you flat out he'd buy them?" Harrington asked.

"Well . . . not flat out, but darned near. If I delivered them an' they was worth the price — fifteen dollars a head I quoted him — he said he'd pay me on the barrel head . . . And you know what, Sheriff?"

"What?"

"Someone got sick down at Agua Prieta an' he went down there to look after them — and my damned horses is runnin' loose somewhere west of town. Fifty miles off by now.

"How did they get out of the corral, Dave?"

Stern's little faded eyes held to Harrington like icicles. "How'd you know they was in the corral?"

"It's my job to know what's goin' on in town. How did they get out?"

"All I know is that they got out. They ain't down there now an' the liveryman said he don't know anythin' about them, an' that big young feller over at the smithy told me he heard free-runnin' horses stampeding westerly from the far side of town the same night Alf here told me someone held up a stage north of Camargo."

Sheriff Harrington refused the offer of a drink, leaned on the table with clasped hands for a moment, then arose, slapped the old stockman lightly on the shoulder and left the saloon.

He had overlooked something. It had occurred to him the day after the robbery but he had not thought of it since. The reason those barefoot horses had been stampeded over the shod horse marks of the outlaws was not simply to obliterate their tracks, but to do it in such a manner that when the outlaws had not continued southward, but had in fact turned eastward into town, trackers reading the sign would simply agree that the tracks would be wiped out and give up, which was exactly what had happened.

They hadn't been wiped out, the outlaws had turned eastward into town, and that meant they had a pre-arranged place to stay — with their loot.

He returned to the jailhouse ostensibly to collect the little pails and after he had done that, had locked the door from the outside and looked in, his prisoner, with more time to consider his situation, said, "You talk to Moro?"

"I told you — he's down at Agua Prieta."

"Oh. Yeah. I forgot."

Harrington continued to stand there looking in. "But I know how he got those horses and why he got them. I don't know for a fact that *he* stampeded them, but I'd bet my life that's what he did. Or maybe some of his kinsmen."

"Why?" asked Hadley, blandly, looking out at the lawman.

"To cover the tracks so's trackers would give up on riders they figured had gone on south."

"Where did they go, Sheriff?"

"Into town."

"You're sure?"

Harrington inclined his head slowly. "I'll find 'em, Mister Hadley. I'll find where they hid out in Camargo and what they did with the loot. It's not that big a town."

At the long look he got from his prisoner Sheriff Harrington added a little more. "I know who two of them were, you and Alba Moro. That's enough to start with . . . Hadley?"

"Yes."

"You got a long night ahead of you. I can use your help."

"In exchange for what, Sheriff?"

"Telling the military authorities when I deliver you to them that you helped me identify the outlaws and recover the loot."

Hadley gazed at the sheriff for a long moment, then smiled a little, stretched out on his bunk, hands clasped behind his head and said, "We can talk some more tomorrow."

"Right now's as good a time as any," stated the lawman, but his prisoner continued to lie there eyeing him through the half droop of eyelids wearing a hint of a smile. "Tomorrow, Sheriff," he said. "Good night."

8

Getting Closer

IT was less the complacent look of his prisoner when he had insisted they could talk tomorrow, than it was the quietly reassured way he had said it; "Not tonight . . . We can talk tomorrow."

Harrington was in the doorway heading out when he saw a familiar figure approaching from the north. He stepped back inside, tossed his hat atop the desk and when Matt Wales walked in the sheriff was waiting.

The rugged coach driver with the somewhat disillusioned expression nodded, blew out a big breath and made an innocuous comment about the condition of the road between Agua Prieta and Camargo.

"Like goin' over a washboard," he

exclaimed, dropping into the chair beside the door. "An' I don't know where they got that driver but he don't know up from down about driving."

Harrington nodded woodenly and waited.

Matt groped for his cut plug. As he was doing this he spoke cryptically. "Alba Moro's got kinfolk down there all right, but ain't none of 'em sick." Wales methodically picked lint off the chewing tobacco. "They got something else down there, an' two of his brothers offered 'em for sale to me because I pretended to be in the livestock buyin' business." Matt paused again until he had his cud pouched into a cheek and was pocketing the plug, then he looked directly at Bruce Harrington. "Thirty head of barefoot horses wearin' a little DS in a circle on their left shoulder. You got any idea — ?"

"Yes, I know who owns them. Get on with it."

"His brothers told me they picked up the band southwest runnin' free."

Harrington lightly scratched the tip of his nose. "Yeah. Runnin' free on a course that'd send them down where Moro's brothers were waiting."

Matt shrugged. "But that's not's all that's goin' on down there. They're expectin' a pack string in a few days. From up here."

Bruce Harrington's brows dropped a notch but he said nothing.

Matt Wales stepped to the doorway, looked both ways and let fly then returned to his chair. "Some *arriero* from up here, Sheriff. Someone up here hired him to pack a load down to Agua Prieta."

Harrington masked his quickened interest by going over to fiddle with the stove before turning with his back to it to ask a question. "Who hired him up here?"

"I never got that far. They was friendly fellers but when I didn't want the horses, they was still friendly but lost their interest in me."

Harrington returned to his chair and

scowled in the direction of the gun rack. "Matt, I'll give you any odds you want that those bullion boxes are still in Camargo. But they won't be if the pack string from here loads up and heads south . . . Patricio Castillo."

"What? Who is that?"

"A packer in Mex town. He's got two strings, one of horses one of Mex mules." Harrington arose again. "Get something to eat and rest for a while. I got to go down to — "

"Where's Hadley? He ain't left the country has he?"

"Locked in a cell," Harrington replied, jerking a thumb over his shoulder to indicate the cell room.

Matt's eyes widened. "When?"

"Not long ago. Got the drop on him down at the livery barn. *El Matador*, remember? Well, Hadley was recognised in Mex town being *El Matador* tossing around gold coins from the stage robbery."

Matt was surprised. "The hell! What — ?"

"Later," the sheriff said brusquely going after his hat. "Get something to eat and rest up."

"Where are you goin'?"

"Mex town. I'll hunt you up later. You did a good job down yonder. Just one question: Where was Alba when you were with his brothers?"

"They didn't say an' I didn't ask. I met them at a cantina, they took me out to some typical Mex corrals, wired together faggots. I never saw Alba. Which was maybe a good thing. If we'd met sure as hell he'd have recognised me."

Sheriff Harrington left the whip in his office taking his time about putting pieces into some kind of order so that he could understand all that had happened since he'd left for Agua Prieta. He was only partly successful.

When Harrington got in among the irregularly positioned adobe residences in Mex town he got some sidelong glances from a few people who saw him, and a more direct reaction from several slab-sided dogs.

The packer's buxom wife was hanging a *bistra* of red peppers in the sun beside the house when Sheriff Harrington appeared. She did not act surprised. She jerked her head in the direction of the corrals out back and continued with her work.

Patricio Castillo was sitting in shade with scraps of pack harness on a scarred old table where he was working. He looked up, nodded, picked up a scrap of cloth to wipe his hands with and said, "That was the man, Sheriff. Did you get him?"

"Yeah. Locked him up." Harrington sat down opposite the big Mexican eyeing the oily harness as he said, "Gettin' ready to head out, are you?"

Castillo nodded also regarding the harness. "Remember I told you it was hard, competing with the stages and wagons? Well, business is picking up a little."

"You're heading south to pick up a load?"

"No. I got a hire to take from here to Agua Prieta."

Harrington relaxed a little. Made a point of examining a mule britching. He had arrived at the point where his next question would — or would not — open the doorway he needed to have opened. Someone in Camargo, not Moro and not Hadley, was going to send the payroll loot south on Patricio Castillo's mules. Disguised, undoubtedly, because the big Mexican showed no sign of nervousness; he had accepted a hire which was all he was interested in. That he thought business was picking up enough for him to comment about that to the sheriff indicated that he had no knowledge of the real cargo he would be packing.

Whoever had hired him knew, and was using the Castillo pack train to get the loot out of Camargo. It looked very innocent, very businesslike.

Harrington tossed the piece of old leather atop the table and quietly asked Castillo what he would be carrying in his packs. Without hesitation and with a direct gaze, the big Mexican replied:

"Hardware for the general store in Agua Prieta." Castillo gave a little shrug. "It's already wrapped. I put some bundles on the scale. You know? A pack has to have equal weight on both sides, otherwise the mule will not be able to balance it well. He will get sores from too much weight on one side."

Harrington understood all this but kept a tight rein as he agreed. "Big bundles?"

"No. Small enough to fit into each *alforja*. They were made that size on purpose. So I could load up without having to re-pack anything."

Harrington retrieved the strap he'd been examining earlier and while running it slowly through his fingers he said, "Who's sending it south?"

"Mister Benton. He's the one who came down here to hire me."

Harrington nodded gently and put

151

the strap aside for the second time. Joshua Benton operated Camargo's general store. He and his partner, Umberto Atocha, merchandised all over the territory. They had a thriving business. The store in Camargo was their headquarters but they supplied other stores in a dozen towns. They also owned several freight wagons which were constantly on the road. Once, they had been in trouble with the U. S. army for sending wagons loaded with weapons and ammunition south into Mexico in support of a revolution, but that had been years earlier. Again, they had been involved in a transfer of melted down church and historic artefacts from Mexico to gold dealers in Albuquerque.

That time they had been within their legal rights. There was no law against moving raw gold from one country to the other. The army did not approve, but that was about all they could do.

Harrington knew both the partners. Joshua Benton was a large, heavy man addicted to good cigars. He was an amiable man with little laughing eyes, a lipless wide mouth, and was well liked. Umberto Atocha was old. He rarely took a hand in running the business now but when they had started out he had been very involved. Now, he lived in Albuquerque, his wife looked after him. He had a private doctor. Harrington hadn't seen Umberto Atocha in Camargo in years. It was rumoured that his health was bad, that he was frail now.

Patricio Castillo was watching his friend's face when he said, "I keep wondering about that *gringo* playing that he was *El Matador*."

Sheriff Harrington nodded. "I'll ask him," he said and pushed up from the table before putting a final question to Castillo: "When will you leave for Agua Prieta?"

"In the morning. Very early. It's getting hot now. I don't like to keep my animals moving with a load when it gets hot."

"The store don't open until eight."

"Mister Benton said he'd be out back at the dock before sun-up. Maybe about four in the morning."

Harrington smiled. "Have a good trip — and Patricio, a favour. Don't mention to Benton that I talked to you today."

As the lawman was walking back around the house heading for his office Patricio Castillo turned on his bench watching him. A little bell had tinkled in his mind some time before: Too many questions, too much trying to act unconcerned. He shrugged and went back to work on the mule harness and kept at it until his wife called him to eat, then he arose, wiped both palms down the outer side of his trousers and dutifully went over to the house.

The sun was beginning to lose its benign splendour. By afternoon it was becoming increasingly fierce. In another month it would be blazing hot all day long, would even arise in the cool dawn full of malign ferocity.

When that time arrived people and animals, knowing there was little they could do against such heat, spent as much time as they could in deep shade. It was one of the unique elements of life on the south desert that while elsewhere on hot days retreat into shade meant a drop in temperatures, sometimes as much as ten degrees, on the south desert the only thing shade provided was protection from direct sunlight; the shade was just as hot, there simply was no fierce glare.

Sheriff Harrington had an excuse to visit the big, busy general store. He needed a couple of conway buckles for some horse equipment. There were women at the dry goods counter, youngsters hovering like insects around the jars of hard candy, and a number of men, including some stockmen from beyond town, making leisurely purchases. It was always cool in the massively-walled adobe building, even without the additional protection provided by an upstairs.

The Camargo Mercantile Company was a landmark meeting place, a dispenser of information, trading post and emporium. Since its inception it had been the best provider of livestock and human supplies on the south desert. As Harrington got his little buckles and leaned to watch the ceaseless activity he caught a glimpse of Joshua Benton, cigar ash on his vest as usual, massive gold chain across the vest, elegant pink sleeve garters above his elbows, jovial smile fixed in place, and looked elsewhere wondering why a man, with accumulated wealth, a very successful business, respect and popularity, would risk it all to master-mind a stage coach robbery.

He returned to the roadway still wondering. On his way to the jailhouse he pocketed the little buckles, spat into the dust and walked in where it was ten degrees cooler — without an answer.

Later, when he got more pails of hash and coffee for his prisoner, Bryce Hadley appeared to have made the adjustment not one outdoorsman in a hundred ever made: He was dozing on his cot as though a cramped little jail cell caused him no problems. But, as Sheriff Harrington well knew, Hadley was the complete master of his feelings.

He roused the prisoner by rattling the keys as he opened the door, put the pails just inside, backed out and re-locked the door.

Hadley smiled as he pushed up off the cot. "Early supper, Sheriff?"

Instead of heeding the question Harrington asked one of his own. "Thought things over yet?"

Hadley's eyes were calm when he replied. "In the morning. Tomorrow we can talk." He picked up the little pails and went back to the cot to perch on the edge of it.

"By tomorrow it will be too late," Harrington said, and caught his prisoner's attention.

"Too late? Why?"

Harrington ignored the questions. He gave just enough information to the prisoner to worry him when he said, "Moro's brothers have those horses. They got 'em corralled down at Agua Prieta."

Hadley, in the process of lifting a spoonful of hash, stopped moving, turned his head slowly and gazed directly at the lawman without making a sound for a long while. Harrington leaned on the cell across the little corridor with arms crossed, waiting. Hadley was not slow; he would know now that Camargo's lawman had the bone in his teeth. If he knew about the horses and Alba Moro's brothers down at Agua Prieta, he probably knew more.

Then he smiled at Sheriff Harrington. "What horses? I didn't know Moro had brothers."

"Sure you did," Harrington replied quietly. "I'll tell you what I think. I think you and your partner made a bad mistake allowing Moro to steal horses when something like that was unnecessary and simply increased the danger for the rest of you."

Hadley went to work on his meal as though Bruce Harrington did not exist. Until the lawman tired of their little game and walked up toward his office, then Bryce Hadley arose, went to grip the straps of his cage and peer after him. If the lawman could have seen his face then, he wouldn't have been so convinced that his prisoner had steel nerves.

As the day wore along Matt Wales appeared, looking scrubbed, fed and comfortable. He was chewing rather than smoking a slim cheroot he'd acquired at the saloon. He did not light it. He never lighted stogies, he was a chewer not a smoker.

They spent a half hour discussing the only situation which was of immediate interest to them both. When Matt mentioned the most recent return of *El Matador*, Harrington shrugged and changed the subject. He'd had time to work out what he hoped would culminate in a finale. He said, "There are two ways to work it in the early morning. Let Castillo get on the road, then swoop down and break open those bundles he'll be carrying, or, be in position out back at Benton's loading dock before sunup and break into them out there."

Matt removed the stogie, studied the wet, frayed end he'd been chewing, and looked up. "If we stop the packer there'll only be him." He plugged the cigar back into his mouth. "If we start something on the dock, sure as hell Joshua Benton'll be out there, and with this kind of a consignment for him to sweat about, he just might have some other fellers back there with him. Sheriff, I never liked takin' chances I didn't have to take, specially since I never could hit a barn from the inside with a sixshooter."

Harrington laughed. "I'll rout you out in the dark then."

"You won't have to rout me out," replied the whip drily. "I been gettin' up in the dark all my life. I couldn't

160

sleep to sunrise if my life depended on it. You know this packer, do you?"

"Well enough."

Wales thought about that for a moment. "What is it they call pack-train men in Mex?"

"*Arrieros.*"

"This here *arriero* won't start shootin' on sight, will he?"

"No. I don't think so."

Wales resumed his pondering and came up with another question. "Seems to me I recollect Benton havin' gun-guards with some of his shipments. You reckon he'll have 'em with the — *arriero*? If you're right this friend of yours will be carryin' most likely the most valuable cargo he ever hauled. I don't know Benton except to nod to, but if he's as careful as I figure he might be . . . "

"We're not goin' to ride down the centre of the road wavin' our hats, Matt."

Wales nodded about that, and screwed up his eyes. "There's a place about five,

161

six miles south of town folks call Point Of Rocks."

Harrington nodded before the other man had finished speaking. "I know the place. Weren't you stopped there once years back?"

"I been stopped there twice. Didn't have much besides a couple of passengers and a sack of mail each time. They robbed me'n the passengers and rode off with the mail sack. Both times." Matt suddenly smiled, a rarity for him. "This time it'll be the other way around. Sheriff; I like that idea!" A moment later the smile winked out and two lines appeared in his forehead. "How many do you figure is involved in this?"

Harrington was not sure. "Hadley, Benton, Moro. Sure as hell Benton wasn't up there when they robbed your coach. When we tracked 'em, Matt, there was four sets of marks."

"Yeah. It's the unknown part that worries me, Sheriff."

Harrington regarded the stage driver

with dry amusement. "You do the worrying," he told Wales. "I'll concentrate on other things."

"What other things?"

"Tryin' to get Hadley to open up a little."

"He ain't done it yet?"

"No. But I stuck a bee in his bonnet a while back. I'll talk to him once more, then lock up for the day and bed down early."

Matt arose, his cigar chewed to a pulp, nodded and walked out. As he was crossing the road he flung the stogie away.

The sheriff settled back to think. Since no one up where the stage had been robbed had seen any of the highwaymen, and since no one had come up with anything about them between then and now, and also because Harrington could only name three men who were involved — and one of them was too fat, too soft and too busy to be riding around robbing stagecoaches — he did not worry, as Matt was doing, even though he thought there might still be two or three unidentified participants.

If, as Matt had surmised, Patricio Castillo would have companions when he left town in the dark tomorrow, it would just about have to be the men Harrington had been unable to account for. While that did not particularly worry Bruce Harrington, it certainly did interest him.

9

A Busy Morning

H E made one more visit to the cell room as he'd told Matt he would; this time his excuse was retrieval of the little pails, but after locking the door he gazed at his quiet prisoner, thought perhaps Hadley's expression and silence might have significance, and said, "You're goin' to lose out all around, partner. In fact you've already become somethin' I don't really need. While you been resting in here I've been picking up information."

Hadley turned his head without rising from the edge of the cot. He studied Harrington's face for a moment before speaking. "What information? You made a couple of lucky guesses is all."

165

Harrington paused, then said one name. "Joshua Benton."

Hadley's eyes almost imperceptibly widened. Only for seconds, then he sneered. "Is this a game? You say a name, I say a name. We used to play somethin' like that when I was a kid."

Harrington had other things on his mind. He turned on his heel and returned to the office, barring the cell room door after himself.

He placed a booted Winchester beside the desk, locked up from outside and started his final round of the day. It was still too early for most of Camargo's business establishments to be closed, and this posed a difficulty he ignored on this particular night. Usually he did not make his final round until after dark, in order to be sure front doors were locked.

Tonight merchants who were careless would have to take their chances, which were not very great. Burglaries were rare in Camargo.

At the saloon he had an encounter he'd have preferred to avoid. The liveryman was at the bar with other men who also saw the sheriff arrive, but while the others only nodded, the liveryman, who had evidently been there some time, went down the bar where Harrington had just ordered a nightcap, settled in and made a conspiratorial wink, "Ain't said a thing," he half-whispered, and an annoyed lawman looked around coldly as he replied. "About what?"

The liveryman's expression changed, his eyes shifted, he faced forward in silence. He knew Harrington's reputation as well as anyone in town, and tonight he had just half-angered the lawman. He cleared his throat and said something about the weather.

Harrington sipped his beer.

The liveryman's discomfort increased. Eventually he went back up the bar to wedge in among some stockmen and order another drink.

Old Dave Stern was still in town. He

arrived at the saloon after supper wearing his customary morose expression. He too took a position beside Harrington, but his company was welcome. Harrington mentioned the old man's horses and Stern put a gloomy look on him as he replied: "I rode out a ways, but hell there's been too much horseback traffic. Even barefoot horses. Only thing I figured, an' I'm not real sure of that, was that they run southwest. Hell, Sheriff, by now . . . " The rancher paused to order a whiskey when the barman came along. After that he left unsaid whatever he might have added, and Harrington yielded a little out of pity.

"I think you'll get 'em back, Mister Stern."

The old man growled a reply. "Mister Harrington, I'm pushin' eighty. In all them years I've never seen what I figured was a miracle."

Harrington could say no more so he bought the old man's drink and departed.

Outside, night was settling, the heat seemed slightly less and there was a cloudless sky. Up at the rooming-house he met Matt Wales sitting on the dilapidated old porch in a tipped-back chair gazing southward toward the far end of town. Harrington dragged up another chair and said, "I got to thinkin' after you left this afternoon. Maybe what we'd ought to do is follow Castillo's pack train from a long way back."

Matt looked around wearing a bleak smile. "Because you figure I could be right about there bein' outriders keepin' an eye on your friend an' his mules?"

"Yes. If I'm wrong — what the hell — the road's straight for ten miles, we can see the pack outfit without being very close."

Matt nodded about that. "An' if there's outriders, we can see them too.

Matt leaned to jettison his last cud of the day. As he was tipping the chair back again, he also said: "It still worries

169

me, just the two of us doin' this."

"Matt, more than two riders down in that country which is pretty much open for miles, would show up like a sore thumb."

"I told you the truth, Sheriff. I can't hit the broad side of a barn with a handgun."

"How about a carbine?"

"I do pretty well with 'em. No marksman, mind you, but about as well as the next man.

Harrington was arising when he said, "That ought to be good enough. Get some sleep, Matt."

The door closed behind the sheriff and Matt Wales continued to sit in the darkness for a while before he too finally turned in.

Camargo had long evenings. As the summer heat got continually less comfortable and people took afternoon siestas to avoid it, it was probably natural for them to be awake long after other people in cooler areas would have retired. Even the luminaries down in Mex town were not blown out until very late. Sheriff Harrington slept like a log. Down the hall in another spartan cubicle, his friend the stage driver did not do quite that well, but he did finally fall asleep. He was far less accustomed to something as likely to prove dangerous than the lawman was. The worst thing he could usually anticipate was breaking a wheel on a run or being kicked by a horse or a mule, things which could eventually be put to rights with no permanent damage.

This other thing, as it wound down to some kind of confrontation, could result in someone getting killed. But he eventually slept, and, as he'd told the sheriff, his eyes popped wide open the following morning in chilly darkness.

Camargo was as quiet as a graveyard. There were no lights, no sounds, not even one of those customary little south desert winds that came stealthily in the night and departed before sunrise.

Matt Wales sat on the edge of

his cot, pulled on his britches, stood up to stamp into his boots, groped for his shellbelt and holstered Colt, buckled them into place and lifted his old hat from a wall peg as he stood by the window considering the night — or very early morning. From habit he sniffed the air, decided that although he would take along his coat, it was not going to be cold very long. The last thing he picked up before locking the room from the dark corridor, was his saddle-booted old Winchester, something he always had with him on drives but something he had not fired, except during hunting seasons, in years.

He paused outside the sheriffs room, heard nothing, speculated about knocking, shrugged and went on out into the cold pre-dawn, cut through a refuse-littered back-lot to the alley and walked southward as far as the livery barn.

Harrington was already down there, bundled in a coat, armed for trouble, and waiting with his seal brown horse. At sight of the whip he arose from the old bench out front and nodded. Neither man said anything as the stage driver turned down the runway to get a horse. The liveryman's night hawk got it for him. He was equally silent. He did not even seem very curious as he handed over the reins and went trooping back to his blanket roll in the smelly little harness room.

As they were mounting out front Sheriff Harrington said: "I forgot to tell you something. Couple hours ago I sneaked down behind the icehouse behind Benton's loading dock and watched them fit the packs into Castillo's mules. I meant to mention that last night — that I was going to go down there."

Matt was rummaging for his plug when he replied: "What time did you get up?"

Harrington wasn't sure. "Two o'clock, I think."

"Have a long wait?"

"Yeah. And it was cold. Anyway, he left town heading south about an hour an' a half ago."

"Any companions with him?"

"No. But I left right after I watched him reach the main road. Benton was there. It must have been a real hardship for him to leave a warm bed in the middle of the damned night."

"Then, if Benton sent riders to keep an eye on him, they could be out there."

Harrington nodded and shot his friend a sidelong look. Matt really was worried.

When they had the pale-looking road dead ahead they crossed over to the east side and continued southward from a distance of about half a mile. Sheriff Harrington was showing more caution than Matt had expected him to show, and that appealed to the stage driver, who had not even ridden with a posse let alone done anything as extraordinary as he was doing now.

The sandy loam muffled sound, there

was no moon and although the sky was riddled with stars, during the predawn hours they were beginning to fade, which meant for all the visibility they made possible, they might just as well not have been up there.

Riding in long periods of silence, coat collars turned up, listening and looking, the pair of horsemen only occasionally halted to listen for sounds made by a number of shod mules over on the road. It was a while before they distantly heard them, and afterwards set their own course and going accordingly.

On the south desert the light of early morning which in other places arrived gradually, greyish blue, rather obscure and lifeless seeming, followed a different procedure. There was a prolonged moment of thin light along the farthest curve of the world, then the sun jumped up like a seed being popped from a grape, and there it was, huge, clear of shadows, ready to begin its relentless course across the roof of the world.

It was unable to overcome the long hours of chilly night for a while, but it eventually would. Springtime on the south desert was very short, summer had always arrived with a vengeance and although most desert inhabitants had evolved ways of avoiding most of the heat, they could not avoid all of it, particularly if they were on horseback travelling across an area where underbrush was minimal, there were no trees, and by afternoon even the big jumbles of huge, ancient boulders, became too hot to hold a hand against.

For a couple of hours as they rode, it was very pleasant. Neither hot nor cold. They shed coats, rolled them and made them fast behind their cantles. Then they aimed for those occasional fields of prehistoric boulders to halt, dismount and watch for movement, behind as well as in front.

Castillo's plodding pack train was

distantly visible. South desert air, until heat-haze distorted it, was as clear as glass. It also made estimating distances very difficult, even for men as experienced at it as Sheriff Harrington and his companion were.

"Mile and a half," Wales conjectured and although Harrington disagreed he said nothing. It did not really matter what the distance was; what mattered was that they had the strong little Mexican mules in sight.

They also stood a long while watching for movement up their back trail. There was none, which was a relief, so they swung up and were preparing to leave concealment when Harrington grunted and raised a gloved hand. He pointed.

What appeared to be two riders were across the road westerly riding in and out of thornpin thickets. They were a mile or so behind the pack train and about half a mile west of the roadbed.

Matt sighed, swung to the ground, stepped in among huge rocks and stood a long time watching. When Harrington said, "Well, well, well," the driver put a jaundiced look in his direction, seemed about to make a retort, then faced forward without speaking.

They were in range country, it was not impossible that the horsemen they were watching rode for one of the livestock outfits, except that the way they were riding, crossing clearings swiftly and using all the concealment they could find while they obviously watched the pack train, made that possibility highly improbable.

"That son of a bitch," Matt growled, referring to Joshua Benton whom he barely knew. "Well, hell, for the kind of money he's sneakin' out of Camargo I guess I shouldn't be surprised. In fact I ain't surprised. Are you?"

Harrington replied without taking his eyes off the distant riders. "No. That's why we hung far back, isn't it?"

Wales ignored the question to say. "Now what?"

Harrington looked around. "We cross to their side of the road, get up to them from behind and have a little talk."

Matt nodded as though he had been afraid the sheriff would say something like that. As they turned toward the horses Matt made a long study of the intervening terrain. It was almost entirely bare of concealing stands of underbrush until they could get at least a mile and a half from their present boulder field.

Harrington did not ride forth, he turned back the way they had come and, with heat rising, finally crossed to the other side of the road about two miles north of where those skulking riders were. When they were over there heading southward Matt got a cud tongued into his cheek. It was a poor substitute for breakfast.

Harrington took the lead. Matt thought he was like a bird dog getting ready to flush a covey. He barely spoke and when he did it was in curt sentences, as in the area where they finally got into the underbrush. "I guess they're maybe a mile ahead." He pointed to the ground where gravelly loam took imprints very well. There were only two sets of tracks.

Time passed, heat increased, the horses broke into a sweat without ever moving out of a walk, and distantly a ring of buzzards in high flight made soaring swoops over something dead down below and ignored everything else.

Harrington eventually halted in speckled, hot shade, stood in his stirrups, nodded to himself, settled down and rode on. Matt remained a few yards back. From here on it was the sheriffs responsibility. Matt had all the faith in the world in Harrington's ability in a situation of this kind, while at the same time, because his nature made it mandatory, he worried about accidents, inadvertencies, a number of the kind of things that could bring disaster even to the best plans of the most seasoned kind of lawman.

The last time Harrington halted he swung to the ground lifting out his carbine as he came down. Matt followed that example without a word. Harrington tied his horse to a wiry thicket, waited, and carrying his Winchester led off on foot.

Only when they had plodded about a hundred yards did it dawn on the stage driver what was happening. He had seen nothing, but he had driven this route dozens of times. About a half mile down-country there was an old stone trough beside the road where coaches and other vehicles halted to tank up their animals. The source of the water was a trickling spring in the midst of another jumble of those huge prehistoric boulders. It trickled day and night through a hollowed out sapling to the trough.

The flow was meagre but whoever had built the old trough had evidently taken this into consideration. He had made the trough twice as large as most roadside troughs were, his reason clearly being that as little water as came through the hollowed log would continue to empty into the trough so that although it would take easily twenty-four hours for the trickle to fill the trough, because it ran continuously day and night it would always be more or less full.

The area around the trough had been trampled clear of growth over the years. The soil was powdery except where water had leaked from hair-cracks at the base of the stone work. There, mud-daubers, whose sting was painful, busily collected mud for nests and woe to the indifferent or unsuspecting critters, two-legged or four-legged, who annoyed them.

It was customary for packers, stagers and everyday travellers to go ahead, scatter the wasps with a hat or a blanket before leading animals up to be watered.

Harrington stopped with sweat running, and sank to one knee leaning on his Winchester. Matt got down beside him. Through a fretwork of dusty branches they could see movement near the trough.

Patricio Castillo had watered his mules and was checking harness and loads before heading out. The big, rawboned dark horse he rode looked almost black from sweat.

As they watched Castillo swung up, whistled at his mules and led off back to the roadway. Harrington lifted his hat, shook sweat off, dropped the hat back down and said, "Well, unless they got camels they got to tank up too."

Matt was worried that they might have already tanked up but did not mention it. He also worried about them being up-country somewhere, because if he and the sheriff were close enough to see Castillo at reasonably close range, so might the other men be.

He was slowly twisting from the middle to look back when Harrington's fingers lightly brushed Matt's arm. There were two riders approaching from the west, as would be the case if the men following Castillo had made a westerly sashay so they could see when the pack train left the area of the trough.

After Matt saw the dusty riders coming in he thought everyone was getting too damned close to everyone else. Now, watching the heavily armed strangers on their thirsty, sweaty horses coming toward the trough, he shifted earlier worries to a new one. Suppose they were professional gunmen?

Harrington did not move but from the side of his mouth he gave his companion another worry. "Damned good thing we tied the horses far back. If they'd come from any other direction they would have maybe found our horses or their animals would have scented them and nickered."

"Luck," Matt Wales said sourly. "But you can't never depend on it."

One of the oncoming riders was a Mexican Harrington did not recognise. The other one he knew by sight. His name was Evan Rhys. The reason he remembered the name was because no one ever pronounced it right and even fewer people had any idea how it was spelt. Evan Rhys became Evan Rice and he hadn't seemed to mind, probably because after a lifetime of difficulties over his name, he was worn down to agreeing with just about any mispronunciation folks chose to use.

Evan Rhys worked for Joshua Benton, sometimes on the freighters, other times taking delivery of livestock, or herding it wherever buyers wanted it delivered. As far as Harrington knew, Rhys was a trouble shooter, and right now he was not sure Rhys wasn't fulfilling just another trouble-shooting assignment with no knowledge about why Benton wanted the pack train watched all the way down to Agua Prieta to be certain it arrived there without trouble.

Time would tell. Evan Rhys and his dark companion drew reins a few yards from the trough, went ahead swinging their hats, then brought up their animals, removed the bridles and stood at ease as the horses drank.

Matt leaned to whisper. "That's one of Alba Moro's brothers. He was one of 'em that tried to sell me those barefooted horses."

10

Heat!

SHERIFF HARRINGTON studied the Mexican, who was a lithe, sinewy man in need of a shearing. He had soft buckskin sewed to the inside legs of his trousers, which was not uncommon among men who rode a lot. Harrington asked the man's name without taking his eyes off the drinking horses or their relaxing riders.

"Justo," Matt replied. "Y'know, the 'J' is pronounced like we pronounce a 'h'."

"Stay here, Matt, keep your carbine up. If either one of them makes a bad move, shoot."

Harrington arose and without a sound walked out into the clearing casually trailing the carbine in his right hand. The men at the trough saw him and very gradually came out of their heat-inspired indolence. The *vaquero* did not know Harrington, but the badge on his shirtfront spoke volumes. The Mexican shot his companion a darting look.

Evan Rhys recovered from surprise and made a crooked little smile. "Howdy, Sheriff. How come you're on foot?"

Harrington returned the smile, but without a lot of warmth, and ignored the question as he said, "What are you doing down here?"

There was no tact in the question and the stare that went with it left no doubt about Sheriff Harrington's sincerity.

Evan Rhys's smile faded, he regarded the larger man from thoughtful eyes for a moment, then shrugged and replied: "Sort of keepin' an eye on Castillo's pack outfit up ahead."

"Why?"

"Why? Well, there's been robberies down here," Rhys replied, sounding annoyed.

Harrington looked at the *vaquero*. "Justo Moro . . . ?"

The Mexican nodded. "Si. Yes."

"You live down in Agua Prieta?"

"Yes. But sometimes I ride up to Camargo, and other places."

Harrington gestured with his Winchester. "Drop the belt gun. Both of you."

They obeyed, but Evan Rhys's face darkly coloured. "What the hell are you doin'?" he growled at Sheriff Harrington, and got a cryptic answer.

"Same thing you're doing. Watching the mule train." Harrington leaned on his carbine studying them. "Evan, Mister Benton send you out?"

Rhys nodded, looking about equal parts hostile and bewildered. "Ain't nothin' very strange about that. I've been out ridin' for him for years. You know that, Sheriff."

Harrington had an enigmatic response. "Yeah, I know that, and now I'm beginning to wonder if I shouldn't have taken more of an interest in your

189

outriding over the years."

Rhys looked steadily at the larger and older man. "Would you mind tellin' me what the hell you're talkin' about?" he growled.

Harrington, watching the Mexican from the corner of his eye, saw the man begin to surreptitiously twist sideways. Instead of addressing the Mexican, Harrington spoke to Matt without taking his eyes off the Mexican. "Drop him if he so much as bats an eye!"

The Mexican's eyes darted around among the thickets. He slowly straightened forward and continued to search for someone in hiding as Evan Rhys spoke to Sheriff Harrington, less hostile now, more bewildered.

"What in the hell is this all about? We was told to watch the mule train in case some damned outlaws tried to interfere with it. What's wrong with that?"

"Nothing," the lawman conceded. "Evan, what did Mister Benton tell you was in Castillo's *alforjas*?"

The stocky man sighed before replying. "All he told me was that I'd meet Justo here, at the lower end of town, an' the two of us was to sort of hang back and watch the pack outfit because there's been highwaymen operatin' down the south road for years.

He didn't say what Castillo was packing down to Agua Prieta?"

Rhys eyed the horses briefly, they had tanked up and were content to just stand for a while. His gaze returned to Sheriff Harrington. "He said it was machine parts for a grist mill, an' if anything happened to 'em it'd take forever to get new ones freighted down here."

Harrington looked at the *vaquero*. "You . . . ?"

Justo Moro smiled and made an elaborate shrug. Too elaborate. Harrington raised his Winchester, held it across his lower body in both hands and cocked it.

Evan Rhys looked stunned. The Mexican's jaw muscles rippled, otherwise

191

he showed nothing until the lawman spoke again. "One more time, Justo. You lie to me an' this'll be as far as you go. What did he tell you was in those pack bags?"

" . . . Mister Benton didn't tell me nothing. Only to meet this man at the lower end of town and outride with him to watch that no one tried to stop the mule train."

Harrington's finger noticeably tightened inside the triggerguard. In a very quiet voice he said, "Justo . . . !"

"Well; my brother and I found some loose horses. He told me we could keep them if I followed the mule outfit until it turned off into the foothills."

Harrington nodded. "Where Alba will take over."

Justo Moro's tongue made a darting circuit of his lips. One thing was becoming more obvious the longer they talked. Sheriff Harrington knew a lot more than Justo had thought he knew when he'd appeared out of the underbrush on foot. He nodded. "Yes.

Where Alba will take over."

"Where will Alba take the packs, Justo?"

"I don't know. He didn't . . . " The words trailed off into breathless silence as Harrington took one step closer, pointed the Winchester to the Mexican's soft parts, and began tightening his touch on the trigger.

Justo Moro stared at the gunbarrel the way a rabbit stares into the lidless eyes of a poised rattlesnake. His tongue made another darting circuit of his lips before he forced his eyes higher, to the lawman's face and the pair of merciless eyes looking icily back.

" . . . Alba will re-pack the bundles onto some of our horses and go east to Alta Miro where he will take a stage two hundred miles to the city of Magdalena. There is a man up there who will put the . . . who will take the *alforjas*."

"Hide them for your brother, Hadley and Joshua Benton?"

Justo sullenly nodded his head.

During this interlude Evan Rhys was watching and listening, wearing an increasingly baffled expression. When Harrington stepped back and removed his finger from inside the triggerguard Rhys said, "What's so valuable about some machine tool parts for a damned grindin' mill?"

Harrington gazed at the crestfallen *vaquero* when he replied to Rhys. "Not parts for machines, Evan, the money stolen from that coach Matt Wales was driving when it got stopped north of town and robbed."

Rhys's eyebrows shot up. He looked at the *vaquero*, but Justo Moro would not look at any of them.

Rhys sounded like a man letting go a big breath after holding it for a long time. "That was more 'n a week ago. You mean to tell me that money's been hid in Camargo until this morning? Hell, they could have got it away — "

"How?" challenged the sheriff. "They'd figure we would search every freight wagon, every stage coach, every

194

buggy, even saddlebags, maybe. So they just let it set, an' when enough time had passed they hired Patricio Castillo to make one of his commonplace trips south."

Harrington turned his head. "Matt!"

Wales walked into view cradling his saddlegun in both hands. He did not look friendly as he halted and considered both Moro and Rhys.

Sheriff Harrington ordered Rhys and Moro belly down. He lashed their arms behind their backs and used their belts to bind their ankles. Rhys looked up. "You goin' to leave us here, Sheriff?"

Harrington sent Matt for their horses. During his absence he told the face-down men at his feet that he had no choice but to leave them; he could not take them along and if he turned them loose —

"For Chrissake roll me away from them damned mud daubers," Evan Rhys said as the fierce little stinging insects began to come in again for their wet earth.

Harrington did that much for them. Rhys looked up darkly and said, "I'm goin' to settle with Mister Benton. The least he could have done was warn us the law'd be interested in them pack boxes."

"I don't think he knew that, Evan, an' if he did, I think he'd have sent more'n just the two of you. Accordin' to what I've heard, there's at least six thousand dollars in Patricio's *alforjas*."

Rhys continued to strain to hold his head off the ground as he sweatily stared at the lawman. "I worked for Mister Benton for years. This here is crazy, Sheriff . . .You goin' to leave us here?"

"Someone'll be along."

Matt returned with their animals and they rode southward following their original strategy of remaining well away from the road, Evan Rhys called after them until his dark companion told him to save his breath, he might need it before someone came along to water horses and freed them.

Rhys was fiercely sceptical of that. "No one who sees us tied like this is goin' to even come close. This south country's got a hell of a reputation for outlaws. Justo, we're goin' to lie out here until we dry up like damned prunes. Folks travellin' down here is suspicious of everyone and everything. Especially if they're told the sheriff did this to us."

Moro flung sweat off before looking at his badly upset companion. "We're not goin' to say the sheriff tied us. We're goin' to say outlaws done it after robbing us."

Matt worried about them too. They were helpless and exposed and something neither the *vaquero* nor Evan Rhys had thought of yet; it wasn't just mud daubers who visited the only source of decent water for many miles. So did desert catamounts, packs of coyotes, tarantulas as large as a man's hand, and ugly, sluggish and deadly-poisonous gila monsters.

Harrington brushed all Matt's mild

recriminations aside. They had lost some time at the trough. He would have been content to make it up by loping, but that made rising dust which walking horses did not do.

When he explained this to Matt, Wales looked a little pained. "What the hell . . . We left the only fellers spyin' on the mule train back yonder. This time of day only travellers are out. It's too hot, Sheriff. We already took care of anyone likely to be troublesome down here. We could ride at a lope for a spell, at least until we see the mules."

Sheriff Harrington did not argue. Neither did he lift his sweating horse into a lope.

The heat was not as bad as it would be in another month; they could sweat hard, which helped, and take their time, which was the best alternative to using up horses on the desert and ending up on foot. They were also concerned about a train of laden mules who would be moving just as slowly.

They came to a rock field with some ragged, half-dead trees around it. Here, Castillo had halted to 'blow' his animals, but not for long because there was no water. Also because, while the immense stones offered shade, like all rocks these stored heat, threw it back in shimmery waves and were hot to the touch.

Matt loosened two buttons on his shirt, re-set his hat far forward to mitigate insofar as he could, sunglare bouncing upwards. Otherwise he squinted for some sight of the mule train. It was not so far ahead that ordinarily it would not have been visible, but enough time had passed on this particular day for the predictable heat waves to be out there. They not only limited visibility, sometimes to less than half a mile, they also distorted the roadbed, the rocks, underbrush, and any movement at all.

What appeared on the southward horizon as a mirage — trees and low hills poised about three feet above the ground — was in fact a sequence of low, uneven leaning hills where trees grew, stockmen ran cattle, and where the road wound its way among them toward more rolling country southward, where the town of Agua Prieta served that more southerly territory as the commercial hub, exactly as Camargo did up north.

They saw Castillo's pack train strung out at what appeared to be no more than a mile or two from the rising, rather wooded country. Matt wanted to close the distance a little and this time Sheriff Harrington — against his judgement — conceded. They loped for a mile, slackened to a walk and were finally able to make out general details up ahead.

The little mules, sweating rivulets, were hiking along showing no signs of tiredness. Patricio Castillo on his big dark horse whose coat glistened, slouched along up ahead. He had a lead shank going back to a particular mule — grey above the eyes — who would have been his bell-animal, if he'd believed in belling livestock, which he did not.

Castillo left the road before reaching the low hills. Harrington and Wales exchanged a look. The mules went dutifully south-easterly toward timber shade and Sheriff Harrington speculated aloud that Patricio knew where there was water, which seemed reasonable, until Matt, squinting unsmilingly as he watched the mules maintain their proscribed distance behind the lead animal, made a dry comment. "Yes; an' maybe not. It's too early to make camp for the night, an' this close to Agua Prieta he wouldn't have to camp anyway. He can be in town before sunset . . . You don't suppose he knows what's in the *alforja*, do you?"

Sheriff Harrington, who had known the packer for years, put an annoyed look upon his companion without saying a word.

They could not follow Castillo without crossing more open country than it was prudent to expose themselves in, so they went due southward until they too, were close to the hills, then turned directly eastward, had to halt in underbrush on the west side until a stagecoach rattled past, then wrinkled their noses, crossed over, got among the trees and halted to climb off, loosen cinchas and as their animals drooped in the blessed shade, they left them and scouted ahead on foot until they heard a mule bray.

One moment later a cougar at least seven feet long from the tip of his tail to his nose went racing past in a flat-out run. He looked neither left nor right.

Matt almost grinned. "Guess he learnt somethin' about mules. They don't run scairt like horses."

Castillo had tethered his mules and was taking them one at a time down into a shallow, broad, rocky arroyo where a warm water creek moved sluggishly. They remained hidden and watched this for a while then returned to their own animals, who were also in need of water. But they hunted up a more distant place to tank them up.

Castillo did not return to the road, he crossed the creek heading south-east, which was not the direction of Agua Prieta. Matt halted beside a dying pine and wagged his head, but after being glowered at the other time he'd voiced his suspicions; this time he said nothing.

Harrington was worried. It was not possible to close one's mind to the suspicion Matt had voiced. It might have been if Castillo had either returned to the Agua Prieta road, or had even paralleled it to get as much shade as possible, but his present course, while continuing to be southward, was eastward, and Agua Prieta was more westerly.

They dogged the mules without difficulty. They did not have to rely on tracks, although they were abundant, they followed the rank scent of mule sweat. Their saddle animals guessed

203

after a while this was the thing to do, and plodded along on loose reins. If those had been horses up ahead whose scent was certainly noticeable, their horses probably would have at least thought about calling to them. But they weren't horses, they were mules.

Castillo did not stop again until he was on the far side of those intervening hills which separated the Camargo country from the more southward, and more purely desert-appearing country.

Where he did finally halt was in the half hidden, shadowy yard of a tumble-down goat ranch where drying red peppers hung gaudily on the front wall beneath an ominously sagging *ramada*.

The sheriff and his companion halted back a short way from the final dip of the last hills. They had a good sighting of the half-hidden little ranch, which was without question very old, and might even have seemed abandoned except for the goats and sheep drowsing in tree shade around the yard and beyond it. And those drying peppers.

Castillo dismounted down there; made no attempt to approach the house where the drying peppers hung, in fact kept his back to it as he led his mules toward the wonderfully cool and pleasant old adobe barn where there were only three or four openings, square as though for windows, except that there was no glass, just square holes.

Bruce and Matt eventually dismounted, stepped ahead of their horses and got comfortable, because whatever the big Mexican packer was doing down there was likely to take a lot of time.

Each time he emerged from the barn to lead another mule inside, when he returned there was no sign of mule or pack harness. Matt speculated that he was indeed, setting up for the night. He also wondered who owned that little place and where they were. If they'd been in the house they surely would have emerged before now. Castillo's animals were going to fill someone's barn, which would be a matter of concern to any rancher.

Finally, the big Mexican emerged from the barn, went to an old trough, tossed his hat aside, stripped off his shirt, leaned down and cupped hands full of cold water over himself. Matt was envious. He'd been sweat-itchy for hours.

Harrington thumbed his hat back, looked sternly down where his friend was dousing himself, and very gently shook his head. "What the hell. He could be in Agua Prieta in an hour. If he stalled all his animals and piled the harness it'd take him until sunset to lead 'em all out and rig them up again."

Wales had his back to a rough-barked old tree while he solemnly watched everything down in the yard. "Want a guess? He's waitin' for someone."

Harrington did not respond, but the vertical lines between his eyes got deeper. "Naw," he eventually said. "It's not what it looks like, Matt. I've known Patricio Castillo since I first came to this country. I'd stake my life on his honesty."

Matt was groping for his plug of tobacco, eyes narrowed nearly closed as he watched the big Mexican down in the yard as he drily said, "Well, right now if I was you, I'd be real careful about sayin' things like that. Partner, if we was to bet, I'd bet you was right back yonder. Castillo knows what's in them pack bags of his, and six thousand dollars in one heap is more'n most Messicans'll make in a lifetime if they live to be a hunnert an' fifty. If he don't know what's in them bags, what in the hell is he doin' down there when he should be on the outskirts of Agua Prieta by now, unless he's waiting for someone?"

The answer to Matt's question came very suddenly to Harrington. Matt was right; the big Mexican was indeed waiting for someone. Back yonder where they'd left Rhys and Alba Moro's brother, the Mexican had said something about being hired to

207

watch the pack train '*until it turned off into the foothills*,' which is exactly what Castillo did. Why hadn't Rhys known that? Maybe because Joshua Benton had not told him. But he *had* told Justo Moro, the brother of one of the men involved in the stagecoach robbery.

The second hunch that sobered Bruce Harrington was when Patricio had told him he was to take a load down to Agua Prieta, that had been the night before he left town with the load. Benton had been out at the loading dock in the morning. He had then told Castillo he was not to go to Agua Prieta, but to this old goat ranch. That last minute change in plans was responsible for Castillo being down there now, waiting for someone. He'd probably not even thought about his conversation the day before with Sheriff Harrington.

The sheriff said, "Gawddamn," and got a surprised look from Matt Wales.

11

The Goat Ranch

SHERIFF HARRINGTON told his companion that whoever was to meet the mule train at the secluded old goat ranch had better show up soon, otherwise dusk would settle, visibility would be down to zero, and their chances of ever finding out what in the hell was going on would be very slight.

Matt chewed, expectorated, peered from slitted eyes beneath the tipped-down greasy brim of his old hat and looked sourly pessimistic. He was about to mutter when a flicker of movement caught his attention somewhere south-westerly from where he was sitting in hot tree-shade atop the rib of land overlooking the goat ranch.

He turned, watched for a long while,

then spoke. "Look to the west. Yonder where there's some dust rising from the direction of the road."

Harrington saw it. "Well, well, well," he murmured with calm concern.

Wales watched without commenting until the horsemen were strung out rather than bunched up, and made a count. "Six of 'em. Now that's nice odds, ain't it, Sheriff? Us two against — "

"They're Mexicans," Harrington said sharply, and when Matt Wales put one of his disgusted looks on Harrington because Mexicans were anything but a rarity the closer one got to the border, the sheriff made another remark and this one wiped the disgusted expression from Matt's face as he put his full attention on the distant riders.

"Matt . . . no pack animals. How are they goin' to move all that weight without pack animals?"

For a while neither watcher said a word, but they both arrived at the same conclusion: The approaching heavily-armed riders were not coming to take delivery from Patricio Castillo, they were coming to take the gold away on Patricio's mules. Harrington shook his head about that. Castillo would never allow anyone to take over his mules, and that encouraged another notion. In Spanish it was called 'dos equis' the double-cross. The longer Harrington thought about it the more he came to believe it wasn't Joshua Benton who was doing the double-crossing, it was those Mexican horsemen. They probably were supposed to take delivery at the goat ranch, but had decided to appropriate everything for themselves, gold, packs and mules, cut Joshua Benton out, and most likely make a run for the border with their loot.

Matt suddenly said, "Your friend the mule-teamster's been in this country all his life. He ought to know there's no place on earth where treachery is fed into folks along with their mother's milk like the south desert. Sheriff, we better start thinkin' of a way to weasel down there before them *vaqueros* get up here." Matt spat out his cud and prepared to stand up. "I don't know what your friend is up to, but if I was him and someone came along an' tried to steal my pack train, I sure wouldn't like it."

As they struck out along the eastward ridge with ample thornpin and dusty, wiry tanglefoot to conceal them from the oncoming riders below, Harrington used his carbine to shove cloying limbs of underbrush aside while he sought a trail down from the heights. Usually, it would have been a game trail, a coyote run, deer trail, some kind of varmint pathway. What he found was a goat and sheep trail with abundant evidence hanging on thorny underbrush that wool and hair bearing critters had made the downward trail the sheriff and Matt Wales finally found.

It was steep. Goats, kept among bands of sheep for a number of reasons, unlike other critters, did not angle around sidehills, but went directly downward. Sheep were not as good at this as goats but they were followers, and actually could navigate steep slopes quite well even though as a rule they preferred not to.

For two men using carbines to push brush away, the steep ascent was troublesome. In places they had to leave the precipitous trail for better footing, but despite their curses the route they followed put them nearer the mesa-like broad expanse of flat country more quickly than a more circuitous ascent would have.

They came down off the slope behind the adobe barn, which kept them from being seen from around front where Patricio Castillo was dozing in shade near the old stone trough and might not have known he was not alone except for the ever-watchful goats, who had been watching the two men coming off the slope for some time before they stood up and, goat-like, made little nickering sounds of interest. The resting sheep responded to the goats' concern by also heaving up to their feet, and, sheep-like, began to bleat and mill in mild confusion.

Patricio twisted to watch for a moment, then sprang up. He had been expecting visitors but not from the direction of that steep hill, so he moved to the barn's doorless wide front opening, picked up his Winchester, and went stealthily down the south side of the barn, halted a foot or two from the corner, and listened.

Harrington halted behind the final thicket before open land and studied the yard, the corrals, the buildings and finally, when Matt edged up, he turned and softly said, "He was over by the trough."

Matt nodded about that and mentioned the alertness of the goats, then jutted his chin in the direction of the barn, which they could approach from behind and, presumably, be out of sight.

Harrington led off. The animals, no

longer upset, watched their progress with keen curiosity, particularly the goats who were inquisitive by nature.

They were half way to the barn's rear doorway when Patricio Castillo stepped into sight on the south side of the barn, trailing his Winchester and looking more surprised than menacing. He had recognised the sheriff before Harrington and his companion got close. Patricio said, "What the hell?"

Harrington faltered but did not stop. "Inside the barn," he said and led the way. Patricio dutifully followed, eyeing them perplexedly but saying nothing. He recognised Matt Wales from having seen him around town, but did not actually know him.

When they got inside where a perpetual fragrant, cool gloom existed, Harrington turned as mules stared over the bottoms of stall doors at them.

"Six riders coming from the direction of Agua Prieta," he told the *arriero*, and Patricio nodded about that. "I was supposed to meet them here.

Mister Benton changed the orders at the loading dock this morning."

Matt Wales drily asked if Patricio was supposed to let the approaching horsemen take his mules, and got a startled — then bleak — look. "Take my mules? What are you talking about? They have pack animals of their own."

Both Harrington and Wales gently shook their heads and Patricio stared at them, looked past out where sunlight brightened the yard, looked back and said, "According to Mister Benton I was to come here, wait until some men met me here, and transfer the pack-loads to their animals . . . How many are coming?"

"Six. Mexicans armed like *guerilleros*."

Again the big *arriero* hung fire as he stared. He finally said, "No pack animals?"

Harrington and Wales shook their heads, and Castillo lips pulled flat in anger. "You think they will try to take my mules?"

"Your entire outfit, Patricio," replied

the sheriff. "Matt and I have an idea they were maybe supposed to meet you here according to Benton's plan — "

"They were, but he said there would be two men with a pack train."

As though there had been no interruption Harrington went on speaking. "But somewhere between where the plan was worked out and now, someone decided to do something different: Take your pack outfit with its cargo and maybe head — not for Agua Prieta but for some place south of the border."

"Double-cross Mister Benton?"

"And you," Wales replied drily.

The big Mexican pulled straight up to his full height and glared. "How close are they?"

Harrington guessed. "Maybe twenty, thirty minutes from the yard." As though reading Castillo's mind, Harrington shook his head. "You'd never make it unless you struck out on your black horse without the mules. Even then I wouldn't bet on your chances."

Castillo was silent for a long time, only the white-knuckled grip on his Winchester offered an indication of the fury that was mounting in his heart.

Finally, he loosened slightly, made a sly smile and said, "All right. At least we know they are coming . . . And they don't know what we know, eh? Well," he made a gesture, "if they don't see the mules in the yard or in the corrals they'll know they're in here, no?"

Harrington did not grin back, but nodded as he replied. "The odds won't be so bad now. What do you think, Matt?"

"I already told you, Sheriff, I'm a lousy shot. Besides, you told me all we was goin' to do was sneak along and watch. Now you're talkin' about a pitched battle."

Harrington eyed his friend. "The door's open, Matt. If you're real lucky you might be able to climb back up that hill and get to your horse."

Wales, who had sworn under his breath all the way down the goat trail, looked out the rear opening in the direction of the hillside and shook his head. "I wouldn't climb back up that damned slope to save my soul."

Patricio went along the north-east side of the yard into the sidehill underbrush to gain sufficient altitude to command a view of the lower country in the direction of the Camargo — Agua Prieta road, and squatted up there with his carbine.

The sheriff and the stage driver remained inside the cool barn to wait. There was no particular plan; Castillo would imitate the braying of a mule, something he'd become very good at over the years. That would let the men in the barn know the Mexicans were within sight of the yard. Castillo would then go back down the yard, but in front of the barn, keeping it between himself and the approaching renegades, and join the others.

Matt was scowling toward the house across the yard where the drying peppers were hanging. It bothered him that despite evidence that someone lived there, so far he had seen no sign of them. He grumbled about this to Sheriff Harrington and got a short comment. "If there was anyone over there sure as hell by now they'd have come out." Harrington was right, but Matt's present state of mind made him more doubtingly sceptical than ever. But he said no more and went toward the west end of the barn to stand in shadows, watching. The Mexicans would appear from that direction.

The first sounds coming from the slightly forested and brushed-over area to the south-west was of laughter followed by a quick rattle of musical Spanish. Matt neither spoke nor understood Spanish. In his trade it was not necessary. Bruce Harrington could get by using border-Spanish but was not comfortable with it. Matt turned with raised eyebrows but the sheriff simply looked blandly back. He hadn't understood what they had heard.

A mule brayed in its see-saw fashion,

brayed twice then became silent. The imitation was good enough to bring the stalled animals to their doors again seeking the source of that sound. Another time Harrington would have been impressed enough to laugh. His only reaction this time was to go toward the front barn opening and wait.

When Patricio Castillo came trotting he was sweat-soaked but grinning. When he was in the doorway he gestured. "You was right, there's six of them — and no pack animals." He dropped his arm, the grin winked out and he put a steady, hard gaze upon the sheriff. "I'll tell you what else; I think they are coming not just to steal my pack outfit and Mister Benton's freight, but maybe to kill me too. Why not, *amigo*? If I was in their boots I wouldn't leave no one alive behind me. Would you?"

Harrington was saved from having to answer by a soft whistle from the rear of the barn.

He and Castillo went back there,

stopped well short of the actual opening and faced the same direction Matt was facing.

The horsemen were working their passage back and forth through dense thickets. There was very little rising dust now, and the mood had evidently changed from the lighter mood of laughter. Perhaps this had something to do with the confounded thornpin thickets. Just as possible, with the yard and buildings in sight, the renegades were no longer riding light-heartedly. What they had arrived here to do required more serious concentration the closer they got.

When they broke clear the men watching from the barn's gloom silently made their appraisal. Six Mexicans on sweaty horses, each saddle rigged with a carbine boot, and each man with belt-gun, made a sobering sight. Also, those dark faces were hard and resolute, as they evidently had to be in order to accomplish what they'd come here to do.

One particular Mexican was short, powerfully thick, bull-necked and thin-lipped. He led the others without stopping after they emerged from the thicket, his course set for the front of the yard where the house was in sight. The waiting men inside the barn heard the horses pass south of them toward the yard. Castillo brushed the sleeves of his companions, jerked his head and started back toward the front opening where they'd have an uninterrupted view of the yard.

When they got up there, but well back from the opening in the gloom, they saw the riders approach the house, swing off and loop reins at a sagging old tie-rack. The bull-built man went over to the house, flung the door open and, with pistol in hand, stepped inside.

He was in there only a moment before returning to the yard as he holstered his sixgun and stood a moment looking around. The goats and sheep were staring without showing any anxiety. One of the Mexicans said, "In the barn, then," and the stocky man nodded, squinted toward the barn and called out.

"Castillo! It's Alba. Are you ready?"

Harrington pulled his eyes off the man he'd rather liked at the Camargo livery barn to look at Patricio, and nod slightly.

Castillo called back in a calm, almost affable voice. "*Seguro*. Where are your pack animals?"

Alba Moro did not reply. He winked at his companions and struck out for the barn. Patricio moved into the barn opening. The more distant Mexicans eyed him woodenly but Alba Moro smiled, an expression Sheriff Harrington recognised; he had been charmed by that smile back in Camargo.

Patricio repeated his question. "Where are your pack animals?"

Alba was half way to the barn when he replied: "We couldn't find them this morning. They got loose last night."

"You can't haul this weight on your saddle horses and ride them too," Castillo said, and Alba Moro smiled again, a very disarming smile as he spoke. "We want to hire your mules to take the cargo south. We will pay you twice what old Benton paid you."

Patricio did not have to raise his voice. He and the former hostler at the Camargo livery barn were only a dozen yards apart. "No, Alba, I don't think so. I agreed to come this far. You was to meet me here with your own pack string. My animals have come far enough for one day."

"Well, *amigo*," Alba Moro replied in that same affable voice. "We could camp here tonight and leave in the morning. That would allow your mules plenty of time to rest."

Patricio's right hand was hooked in his shellbelt, as was his left hand. Alba Moro stopped several yards out, both hands at his sides as he smiled. "Maybe when he get to Agua Prieta my brother will have caught our animals and brought them back. Patricio, it's only a few miles to Agua Prieta. You take the cargo that far, that's all. It won't be hard on your mules."

Harrington saw two of the men across the yard slowly turn their backs toward the barn, and brushed Matt's sleeve with his fingers. Matt had also seen the stealthy manoeuvre and nodded without taking his eyes off the riders over in front of the house. Both men raised their Winchesters from deeper in the barn; both of them were worried about Patricio. He was standing in plain sight facing Alba Moro who was no longer smiling.

Alba Moro spoke quietly without taking his eyes off Patricio Castillo. "Justo is behind you somewhere, Patricio, with him behind you and six of us in front of you . . . *Oje compadre*, all I'm asking is that you let us pay you twice over to take the cargo down toward Agua Prieta. That's all."

Patricio stood like a statue looking from Alba Moro to the five men over in front of the house, two of which had their backs to him. He finally made a little fatalistic shrug of the shoulders.

"Alba, I don't like this. You was supposed to come here with your own animals."

Moro threw his arms wide. "I already told you — they got loose in the night, otherwise we'd have brought them."

"You was supposed to come here with the pack animals and one other man besides yourself. You come here with five men and no — "

"Jésus María," exclaimed the burly man, speaking angrily in Spanish. "Look you: We have to use your mules and we have to go quickly. Patricio, be tranquil. Only do as I say. Otherwise . . ." Alba shrugged, the two men across the yard came around slowly with cocked sixguns in their fists.

Castillo considered the pointed weapons, the hard, cruel faces across the yard, returned his attention to Alba Moro and made that little shrug of resignation again. "All right. Answer for me one question, friend. You came armed with more men, for what? Do you know what's in the packs? Parts for someone's mining machinery. But now I wonder ... You don't act like someone who is supposed to take over the parts of a machine for *Señor Benton*."

Alba Moro's patience had run out. He regarded the *arriero* from cold dark eyes. "Are the packs in the barn?" he asked, and when Alba turned to motion for his companions to approach, Patricio told him the packs, the harness, the heavy *alfojas* and his mules were indeed in the barn, then Patricio stepped to one side of the wide barn opening as though to allow Moro and his men to enter.

One Mexican remained with the head-hung, dozing horses. The other four started across the yard. The two men with cocked handguns had eased down their hammers but had not holstered their weapons.

Alba Moro did not take his eyes off the big *arriero* as he walked up to within fifteen or twenty feet of him. He was wearing that beguilingly warm and affable smile again. He said, "Don't worry. We will pay you very well and no one will make the mules work hard. *Compañero, Señor Benton* would approve. What else could we do — our mules got away in the night and he wants that cargo taken care of. When you get back he will understand. All right?"

Patricio did not have an opportunity to reply. When Alba stopped speaking and turned his head toward the shadowy interior of the barn he saw Sheriff Harrington and another man kneeling with saddleguns snugged back and aimed squarely at him. He was so surprised he made a little choking sound in his throat, and two seconds later gave a huge bound toward Castillo to put the *arriero* between himself and those two aimed Winchesters.

He did not scream a warning, but none was necessary. When the Mexicans approaching the barn saw their leader jump so suddenly for shelter, they scattered like quail.

12

Dead Men

THE first shot came from somewhere north of the barn, probably
intended for Patricio Castillo.
Instead it struck Alba Moro low in the
back. He fell, but slowly, grimacing in
pain as he attempted to face the man
who had shot him.

It wouldn't have helped; the gunman
was not visible, but gunsmoke rising
into the still, hot air indicated that he
had got as far as the nearest thick stand
of underbrush. Patricio drew and fired
in that direction, but leading slightly to
the west. No one fired back as Patricio
sprang clear of downed Alba Moro to
fade into barn-gloom as other men in
the yard, fired.

A small keg inside the barn on the
north side took a direct hit and sent

slivery wooden slats in all direction. Another shot, also coming through the doorless front opening, hit a suspended *olla* which broke spraying water.

The men inside the barn had no visible targets even though each shot sent a gust of dirty greyish smoke into the air.

The mules panicked in their stalls adding their kicking and plunging to other sounds. Patricio called to them in Spanish. He might just as well have spoken soothingly to them in Chinese.

Alba Moro's men fired intermittently, more, it seemed, to test the strength of the enemy than in hopes of hitting anyone protected by the massive bulk of the adobe barn. They were also prudent — or experienced — men because, except for an occasional puff of dirty grey gunsmoke, they were invisible.

Sheriff Harrington was impressed with Patricio Castillo's firing tactic. It too, he thought, indicated experience. Patricio would lead what he assumed would be a moving gunman who, after firing, did the natural thing — moved away from the place from which he'd fired.

How Castillo arrived at which direction to lead an assailant Harrington could not guess and in fact he never did get an explanation, but the fight had been in progress no more than ten minutes when it appeared to Harrington that there were no longer five men out there. It was during one of the brief lulls when he fired blind to attract return-fire, that he decided there were three renegades where there had been five.

Matt Wales was concentrating on what he was doing. His expression was bleak but there were also signs of willingness. He stopped firing once to reload, looked at Bruce Harrington and shook his head. It was too noisy for conversation. He was raising his weapon again when a gunshot came from out back through the rear barn opening and Matt winced, dropped flat and rolled.

Ahead of him the *arriero* was already

moving back, keeping as close as possible to the south wall as he passed Matt.

If whoever'd had the presence of mind to take advantage of the preoccupation of the men in the barn with their adversaries out front, to sneak around back had been either bolder or a better shot, he would probably have blown Matt's head off.

Having exposed his position, he no longer had any advantage. Harrington watched Patricio stalking him through barn gloom.

Beyond the barn to the rear there was no shelter. It was the same open ground Harrington and Matt had crossed to reach the barn earlier, and had been seen by the *arriero*. If the man who had tried a back-shot hadn't run like a rabbit after firing through the rear barn opening, or had ducked around the south side of the barn, Castillo would see him.

Patricio got flat down, removed his hat, pushed his gun-hand ahead, eased his face out at ground level, swept the area with a hasty glance, shoved back and got to his feet. The *vaquero* was not in sight.

Harrington arose, crossed to the south side deep in the barn where he could not be seen from out front, entered the stall of a snorty, aware-eyed mule, eased past to one of those glassless square window-holes, paused a moment as the gunfire brisked up again, and when the ensuing lull arrived he leaned quickly to look outside along the wall from back to front.

There was a man flattened against the wall a foot or two from the south-west corner. He was holding a cocked sixgun shoulder high, his head turned toward the back of the barn as though he expected to be stalked from that direction.

Harrington was easing up his sixgun when two things happened simul-taneously. Gunfire broke out again from the direction of the house. Matt replied to it. At about the same time the man who had flattened against the wall turned his head in Harrington's direction, possibly distracted by the gunfire from across the yard. He saw Harrington. For seconds they stared at one another, then Harrington shoved his sixgun through the square hole at about the same moment another gun, this one from inside the barn, added to the deafening exchange up front.

The man hastening desperately to shoot at Harrington went forward off the adobe wall as though struck in the back by a giant hammer. He lost his handgun and was leaning back, bow-like, as his legs began to give away. He seemed to be trying to face around toward the man who had shot him, but never quite made it before he fell on his side and rolled, then became still.

As suddenly as the latest fusillade had began, it stopped. Harrington left the stall, looked up where Matt was seeking targets with his handgun, his shot-out carbine lying in the dirt, then looked in the opposite direction down where

Patricio was leaning on a stall door, shaking his head. He had evidently reloaded because when he saw the sheriff looking at him, he leathered his handgun and walked forward.

The silence ran on until it became nearly as unsettling as the gunfire had been. Harrington thought he heard horses and hastened past Castillo toward the rear opening to look out there.

He caught no more than a quick glimpse of what he thought was two horsemen charging recklessly through the underbrush riding low in their saddles.

Patricio spoke from beside him. "Why didn't you shoot that man against the wall? He was going to kill you."

Harrington replied still straining to see the fleeing riders. "I was raising my gun."

Patricio shook his head, said no more and joined the sheriff in watching dust banners streaming in the direction of the Agua Prieta roadway. In an almost casual tone he said, "Two escaped. Four didn't."

Matt Wales did not abandon his vigil of the yard even when he knew the *arriero* and the sheriff were looking out the rear doorway and talking about the fight ending. Matt did not arise until the other two walked forward and joined him.

He had a torn upper sleeve and blood showing where a ricocheting slug had sliced across his upper arm. He ignored the injury as he leaned to pick up his Winchester, lean it against a stall door and spit cotton. He'd been thirsty even before the skirmish. He was doubly thirsty now and covered with dust, gunpowder stench and sweat.

He was eyeing the big Mexican as he said, "That was like shootin' at shadows. How many rode off?"

Harrington's reply surprised Matt. "Two."

"Well hell we didn't nail four, did we?"

Patricio Castillo was gazing out into the silent, empty yard. "You can walk out there," he said, and grinned a little.

Wales saw no humour in any of this. He looked disdainfully at the *arriero*, then switched his attention to Bruce Harrington. "That could be a trick; two leavin' to make us think it's safe to go outside, an' another one or two waitin' to nail us."

Harrington began shucking out spent casings and plugging in charged loads. He was fairly sure the two who had fled were the only survivors but did not say so. As he closed the gate on the last bullet and leathered his sixgun he looked at Patricio Castillo, a direct, quizzical gaze. He'd seen several things that made his years-long opinion of the Mex town mule packer inaccurate. One thing was the way he'd lead a target before firing. Another thing was the way he handled a sixgun — like someone very experienced in using guns. Finally, there was Castillo's absolute calm and total confidence. Too professional, too calm. He said, "Patricio, do you really believe Alba came out here with gunmen to steal a cargo of machine parts from you?"

Castillo's calm dark gaze lingered on the sheriff when he replied. " . . . Maybe not. I wasn't more than a mile and a half from town when I saw a little skiff of dust behind me. Riders, but they weren't using the road. I didn't ever see them but they were back there." The big Mexican shrugged. "Travellers use the road. Skulkers stay clear of roads. By the time I got to the stone trough and they hadn't tried to come up close, I figured they were following me but with no intention of stopping me. Well, why would that be?" Patricio shrugged again. "Because they were interested in my *alforjas*? They were keeping an eye on me, maybe to make sure I followed orders, maybe to make sure no one tried to rob me. Of what? Pieces of mining machinery? . . . Something else?"

"Did you look into the bundles?"

"No, but while I was loafing over at the trough before you came, I was thinking of doing that. Tell me, Sheriff, am I carrying machine parts?"

"No. The gold and currency stolen from Matt's stagecoach. The army payroll."

Castillo's eyes widened. "Joshua Benton was in on that?"

Harrington nodded his head. "And that feller you nodded about when he and I walked past you. And Alba Moro. Maybe more, I don't know yet."

Castillo twisted to gaze at the mound of pack equipment he had removed from the mules and dumped carelessly aside. He said nothing for a while, not before returning his gaze to Sheriff Harrington. "Those men who were following me — knew?"

"I think one of them did. He works for Benton. The other one is the brother of Alba. We left them tied behind the stone trough."

Castillo stood a while as though listening, then walked far enough forward to look at Alba Moro. While his back was to Wales and the sheriff he said, "Was his name Justo Moro?"

"Yes."

Castillo faced around. "I know him. And his brother. They are thieves. Sheriff, could he be loose by now?"

"Probably. Matt and I figured someone might come up to the trough to water animals and see those two lying there and turn them loose."

"Why didn't you set them afoot? Sheriff, Justo Moro will be out there somewhere. He's a dangerous man."

Matt Wales did not look cheered by this conversation but right at this moment his foremost concern was water. He went up to the front of the barn, passed back and forth several times then stepped out into the sunlight. Nothing happened so he struck out for the house.

Harrington and Castillo watched his progress, not worried just interested.

242

When he reached the house and entered it Patricio jerked his head and led off toward the nearest thicket north of the barn. They found a dead man half-hanging in a flourishing big thicket. Castillo shrugged and turned away, leading off around the yard easterly and halted between a small shed and the house. There was another dead man over there. He had evidently been shot while easing around the corner of the shed to fire down through the barn.

Harrington had not fired in this direction during the fight and after being led to the exact spot where the renegade was lying, he doubted very much if Matt had nailed him. But Patricio was moving again and the sheriff had no time to ask questions.

The third dead renegade was flat on his back where impact had knocked him off the roof of the house where Matt had gone in search of water. Harrington definitely had not fired at this man. He'd had no idea one of them would be atop the house.

Patricio went to the house, called, Matt called back and was holding a dipperful of water when his companions walked in. He offered them water from an oak water barrel. They drank, Matt drank last and was draping the dipper from a wall peg when he said, "Cupboards are full, Sheriff. Someone sure as hell lives here."

The *arriero* nodded. "Yes. An old man and his wife. They have lived here since I can remember. They make cheese and sell meat. They are the grandparents of my wife."

Matt, remembering the indifferent attitude of Castillo when he arrived in the yard, said, "You knew they weren't here?"

"*Si*. They arrived at my house up in Camargo yesterday to spend a few days with my wife. They are all the family she has." He turned. "Sheriff, what about my cargo?"

Harrington had thought about that. Had, in fact, studied the position of the sun. Now, he said, "We'll help you rig out. If nothing else happens today we'd ought to be able to get back to Camargo before dark."

Castillo clearly had more to say, but kept it to himself until they were back at the barn harnessing his mules. Then his first question had to do with Harrington's intentions about the money.

Answering that was easy. "Lock it in the jailhouse safe, set a guard over it day an' night, and send someone for the army."

Matt was already thinking about that steep hill he did not want to climb to get back to his saddle animal, but when Castillo said, "What about the dead outlaws?" Matt's attention returned to his companions. He scowled. "There aren't no shovels in here. Besides, if we got to hang around this place for as long as it takes to dig four graves we won't get back to Camargo until tomorrow."

Sheriff Harrington thought they should bring them into the barn, cover them, and let the law down in Agua Prieta, the closest town, know where the corpses were.

No one argued. After getting the mules ready to travel they brought the four dead men, including Alba Moro, to the barn lined them up side by side in the centre of the earth floor, scouted up some old pieces of canvas to cover them with, and led the mules outside.

Their lodestone was Castillo's big black horse. Mule-like they had long ago formed a solid attachment for the horse. They watched everything it did and when Castillo swung up with a loose shank on one greying mule, the other mules were ready to follow.

Matt and the sheriff walked behind the last mule. When they entered the underbrush and started to climb Matt cursed under his breath. Before he reached the topout he had made a solemn promise to himself. Never again, as long as he lived, would he become involved in anything that had to do with the law.

246

Sheriff Harrington, who had to be as tired and hungry as Matt was, showed no signs of either discomfort once he was back astride his gelding. He rode ahead. The discussion about Justo Moro back at the goat ranch made him a little wary. He did not know Justo Moro well enough to know whether the man would cause trouble ahead, but he did know that if Alba's brother had any idea of the real value of what was in Castillo's *alforjas*, the temptation would certainly be great, even in the face of the kind of odds he would encounter if he tried to stop and rob the mule train.

He saw three travellers on horseback, watched them pass leisurely southward. He also saw a stage coach and a snail-paced freight wagon, otherwise the road north seemed perfectly safe.

When they got back to the stone trough none of them expected to find the men Sheriff Harrington had left there to still be around, and they weren't.

The animals had been without water a long time. The men waited patiently for them to fill up. There was little said but each of them watched the road in both directions. When they struck out again even Matt Wales was beginning to feel better. His mood lightened with each mile they traversed but he also kept his eyes moving. He was not convinced that Joshua Benton's hired man might not have decided to throw in with Justo Moro in some attempt to ambush the pack train.

They were only a few miles south of Camargo when four riders appeared atop a low landswell to the east watching their progress. Matt's anxieties returned in a rush. Patricio said nothing, neither did the sheriff, but they slouched along watching the distant horsemen. Patricio finally did what seemed to come naturally to him, he shrugged as he said, "Why would anyone who wanted to rob a pack-train, ride atop a hill in plain sight?"

Neither of Castillo's companions

replied. They were watching the motionless horsemen in the middle distance.

Castillo may have been right, because the distant riders allowed the train to pass northward, making no move to ride toward it down off their slight elevation.

Harrington had rooftops in sight before abandoning his private thoughts, which had to do with Camargo's successful merchant, Joshua Benton, and Bryce Hadley. Alba Moro was out of it. Possibly his two brothers were involved. Certainly they were horse thieves.

Harrington had considered the possibility of more than four or five people being involved in the robbery and the subsequent attempt to smuggle the stolen money out of Camargo, but he had no actual proof of this. Of Bryce Hadley, Benton and Alba Moro he was certain. About others, he was not convinced, and he was not unconvinced; but it had seemed to him there certainly had to be at least one other man. Whoever had driven these barefoot horses over the tracks of the escaping road agents had certainly and deliberately, driven that loosestock the way it had been done to cover tracks.

He wondered whether Hadley had been softened up enough yet to answer questions. As for Joshua Benton, Harrington could imagine his reaction to being arrested and charged with complicity in a stage robbery.

Patricio calling from back a dozen or so yards put an end to the sheriff's speculations. He wanted to know whether to enter town down the centre of Main Street where everyone would see them unload the *alforjas* out front of the sheriff's office, or go over to the west-side alley and approach the jailhouse from back there.

Harrington led off in the direction of the alley. He did not expect to reach the jailhouse unseen, nor did he. Both the liveryman and a friend of his stood on the alley barn-opening watching. Nothing was said; the men did not even nod back and forth.

There were other spectators, mostly by accident and from the rear doorways of stores, but there had been no intention to keep the arrival of Castillo's pack outfit back in town a secret.

As they were tying up out back Matt said: "Fifteen minutes is all it'll take. Then the whole darned town will know."

Harrington agreed with this as he helped carry bundles from the *alforjas* inside his office where he knelt to work the combination on his steel safe and place each heavy bundle inside as Matt and Patricio brought them in from out back. He slammed the door, spun the tumblers, stood up facing his companions and said, "Take care of the mules, Patricio. Matt can take care of our horses. Then I'd like you gents to meet me back here in the office in a couple of hours. Right now I got to find Joshua Benton before he hears that his pack train returned to town, and disappears."

But before beginning his search for the storekeeper he found an itinerant cowboy out front of the café and paid him a silver dollar to ride to Agua Prieta and inform the authorities that there were four dead men in the adobe barn of an old goat ranch north-east of Agua Prieta about two or three miles.

13

The Return to Camargo

JOSHUA BENTON had been in his cubbyhole office at the general store when a casual stroller entered and during the course of purchasing a sack of Durham tobacco mentioned to Benton's clerk that he had seen Patricio Castillo's mule train enter town a short while ago from the south.

Benton leaned back off his desk, took out his big gold watch, sprung the face open, consulted the delicate little hands, snapped the watch closed, without thinking shoved a cold cigar butt into his mouth and stood up. He hesitated only until he heard boots echoing over the oiled wooden floor in the direction of the roadway, then left the office, approached his clerk and said: "Who was that customer?"

"Rhys."

"What's he doing in town?"

The clerk looked blankly at his employer. "Ain't he supposed to be? Far as I know he's been around all day."

"Where did he go?"

The clerk shrugged. "Just walked out. Maybe up to the pool room. That's where he hangs out when he ain't working. Is something wrong?"

Joshua Benton turned away without answering, stood in the roadway just beyond his front door, saw no sign of his hired man, flung the cigar away and turned in the direction of the pool room, which was two doors south of the saloon. He was passing one of those narrow openings between two buildings called a 'dog trot' when Sheriff Harrington stepped out and smiled.

Benton gave a slight start as the larger man blocked his advance and said, "Mister Benton, I'd take it kindly if you'd take a little stroll with me."

"What for? Sheriff, I'm busy right now . . . " Benton flinched as an iron grip closed on his upper arm. He would have twisted sideways but Harrington's grip kept him from moving.

"Just a little walk," said the lawman mildly, and turned the shopkeeper with a rough shove. "Over to the jailhouse. Walk natural an' stay ahead of me."

Benton's colour deepened as he started to protest. Harrington gave him a slight, hard punch from behind over the kidneys. "Just walk, Mister Benton. I want to show you something."

Benton walked.

There were people on both sides of the road who paid no attention to the storekeeper and the lawman, but one man sitting on an old bench a couple of doors south of the jailhouse, hat tipped down over a beard-stubbled face, watched them from slitted eyes. As they entered the jailhouse he leaned, sprayed amber into roadway dust, shoved back his hat and arose. A yardman for the stage company walked past carrying broken harness over one shoulder. He nodded at the beard-stubbled man and stopped to talk. "Matt, the boss's been lookin' high an' low for you. One of the other drivers got sick yestiddy. The boss wants you to fill in."

Wales considered the yardman briefly before saying, "You tell him for me that when he fired me, we parted ways for good. Let him drive the coach himself."

Matt moved toward the jailhouse leaving the yardman standing like a statue staring after him.

When he walked in both Sheriff Harrington and Joshua Benton looked up quickly. They'd been in the middle of speaking. Matt gave each of them a sour look and sat in the old chair beside the door.

Harrington wasted a moment eyeing the stage driver, then did as Patricio Castillo did so often, he shrugged and faced Joshua Benton again as he said, "Like I just said, I got a friend of yours in the cells."

Benton was angry. "What friend?"

As Sheriff Harrington replied he arose, stepped to the steel safe and while working the tumblers replied to the storekeeper. "Bryce Hadley."

Benton said nothing. He and Matt both watched Harrington put one of the cloth-wrapped bundles atop his desk and unwrap it. Someone, probably Joshua Benton, had wrapped the money with considerable — almost loving — care. The wrapping had been wound so that the coins would not rattle even on a mule's back.

Matt stared at the money. So did Joshua Benton, but his fleeting look of consternation was immediately followed by an expression of defiance. "Well," he exclaimed. "What is it, where did you get it?"

Harrington sat down gazing across the room. He'd never thought Joshua Benton would cave in. "It's the loot from Matt's stagecoach that was robbed a while back. Where did we get it? From Patricio Castillo, after we got back to town from that little isolated goat ranch you told him to head for and wait for someone to come and get it from him . . . Mister Benton, they came, six Mexicans armed for war. They didn't have any pack animals. They meant to take Castillo's outfit, shoot him, then head for the border as fast as they could." Harrington smiled again. "One of them was your partner, Alba Moro. He was going to double-cross you, Mister Benton, take it all for himself."

Joshua Benton's expression was difficult to read, but he most certainly was speechless because he sat staring at the stolen payroll for a long time, glassy-eyed and breathing shallowly.

Harrington re-wrapped the money and returned it to the safe. As he turned back toward his desk he said, "You got any idea what the army'll think about outlaws who steal one of their payrolls?" As he sat down again the sheriff also said, "What I can't understand for the life of me is

— hell — you got a thriving business, a big successful store; why would you engineer a stage robbery? That's what two-bit renegades do."

Benton remained silent, his colour was draining. He went to the water bucket, drank a dipper full and returned to bench, still silent. He looked every day of his age.

Harrington arose, picked up the copper keyring and went over to the cell room door. As he was inserting the key he said, "Alba's dead. Him and four of his *guerilleros* or whatever they were." Harrington paused with the door partially open. He looked at the sweating storekeeper. "You been down here longer'n I have, Mister Benton. You know how these people are; if they figure they're not goin' to get up again they got to confess."

Harrington stopped short of lying and went down into the cell room. Matt was examining his plug, sitting relaxed and comfortable beside the door. He spoke softly and slowly. "Mister Benton, like the sheriff said, they figure they're goin' to die they want a priest. Well, there wasn't one down there where we fought it out with 'em. But Alba wouldn't cash in without a clean soul would he?"

Benton spoke harshly. "What did he tell you?"

Matt continued to study his cut plug. "Everything. How you organised the robbery, let the money cool off until you figured it was safe to send it out of the country. Even how Alba was goin' to take it up north for safekeeping."

Joshua Benton let go a loud, rattling breath and leaned to arise. Matt had the plug in his left hand, his sixgun in his right hand. "Sit down," he said, and waited a couple of moments until he was obeyed, then carelessly leathered his weapon and went back to examining the tobacco plug.

"Tell me something, Mister Benton," the stage driver said as he finally decided which edge of the plug to bite into. "Did Alba's brother know what was in them pack bags?"

"You mean Justo?"

Matt grinned from ear to ear. "Yeah. Justo."

"I didn't tell him. Nor did I tell Rhys."

"Well, I think someone did, Mister Benton. An' if it wasn't you, then I'd guess it was Alba, an' if that's true, why then my guess is that Justo was supposed to help the others ambush and kill Castillo."

"My orders were to protect the mule train until it got to the goat ranch where Alba would meet it and take over from Castillo."

Matt continued to smile. "That's exactly what happened — except that the sheriff and I caught Rhys and Justo Moro at the old stone trough and left them tied while we went on over the hills down to that little goat ranch. What I'm wonderin' now is: Where are Rhys and Justo Moro?"

"Rhys is here in town. He was in the store not more'n an hour ago."

"How about Justo?"

"I don't know. Maybe Evan knows but I certainly don't. He was in the plot with his brother to steal the money?"

Matt's grin widened until it seemed his face would split. He mimicked the sheriff. "Well, well, well. Now then, you knew it was the loot an' not no machine parts. Hell, you just as good as told me you knew when you asked whether Alba's brother might have been in the double-cross with Alba. You didn't say machine parts, you said — *the money*."

Harrington returned from the cell room. Both men looked quickly at him, but he was expressionless as he crossed to his chair, sat down, planted both elbows atop the desk and looked steadily at Joshua Benton.

The stage driver finally asked a question. "What did he say?"

Harrington turned his head, hung fire for another moment then replied. As a matter of fact all Bryce Hadley had done was complain bitterly about not being fed nor allowed to go across the alley to the outhouse. When Harrington had told him he had Joshua Benton in the office, with the stolen payroll in his safe and that while Alba Moro had tried to double-cross the others and steal the loot for himself, he had got killed during the attempt, Hadley had stood in the centre of his cell glaring out at the sheriff as he said, "What the hell do I care? You left me in here to starve. Mister, I wouldn't help you if you was the last man on earth."

Harrington phrased his words carefully. "He got a load off his chest. He's as mad as all get out."

Before either of the other men could speak, Harrington faced the merchant again and spoke quietly. "He didn't know about Alba double crossing you an' him. He got pretty mad."

Benton spoke harshly. "You got to prove all this, Sheriff. So far I haven't seen no proof of anything, except maybe that Alba tried to rob Castillo's pack train. An' that don't concern me nor Hadley."

Matt rolled his eyes and told Harrington almost word for word what Benton had said about 'the money' in Castillo's pack bags instead of machine tools.

Benton, definitely in a defiant mood now, turned on Matt. "Your word against mine. You're nothin' but a stage driver. I'm known all over the territory. I've done business with anyone worth doin' business with. I own property, a successful business. I got — "

"Mister Benton," the lawman interrupted to say, "I'm goin' to lock you up. I got things to do. You can't argue with a stone wall." Harrington arose but did not pick up the copper keyring. He instead herded the merchant into his storeroom, took down a set of irons and an Oregon boot and under Matt's approving gaze and Benton's outraged sputtering, made the merchant fast to a large steel ring imbedded in the east wall, a remnant of days when there had been no steel-strap cells, only the storeroom to serve as the area of confinement.

He locked the door after himself, ignored Benton's racket behind the door and asked if Matt had seen old Dave Stern whose horses had been used to cover shod-horse tracks the night of the stage robbery.

Matt had. The old rancher was playing poker at the saloon. He had said aloud within Matt's hearing that first thing in the morning he was heading for home.

They went up there but the rancher had departed. No one knew where he'd gone but it was a fair bet he'd be either at the pool room, the café, the general store or the livery barn.

He was at none of those places. Fifteen minutes of scouting located him at the saddle and harness works having a leisurely cup of black java with the harness maker, an equally as aged, grainy-skinned individual who had been a stockman for three times as long as he'd been a harness and saddle maker.

When Harrington and Matt walked in the older men eyed them dispassionately. Coffee was offered, which they declined, and the sheriff told Dave Stern where his horses were, the name of the men who had corralled them down at Agua Prieta, and volunteered to write a note to the law down at Agua Prieta requesting a posse go with old Stern to recover his horses.

Both the older men brightened a little. Neither got very enthusiastic; both were past the age where enthusiasm had any part in their lives.

Dave Stern returned to the jailhouse with Matt and Harrington, waited until the letter had been written, which seemed to take an inordinate amount of time, sealed and handed over, then the old man shoved out a calloused, mottled hand, shook and departed.

Matt was eyeing Harrington quizzically. "It wouldn't have taken me dang near fifteen minutes to — "

"It would have if you'd told the law down yonder why those Mexicans were killed at the goat ranch, and that if Justo is down there, he's wanted up here for horse theft an' I'd take it right kindly if he'd send the son of a bitch up here in chains." Harrington reached for his hat as he finished speaking.

Matt returned to the saloon with the sheriff where he stood the first round, Harrington stood the second round and a gangling, tall man with a prominent adam's apple came in looking around, found Harrington, sidled up to him and spoke in a voice lowered so other patrons would not hear when he said, "Sheriff, there's someone in your storeroom tryin' to tear the place down. I was walkin' up the alley. He was cussin' and slammin' things around."

Harrington thanked the informer, turned slowly toward Matt Wales, and smiled as he offered a slight salute before downing his liquor. Afterwards he said, "Matt, I think we got the important ones. In fact we got four more'n we bargained for. But there's still a loose one . . . Unless it was Justo drove the barefoot horses around to cover tracks."

Matt made a shrewd guess about that. "Don't hold your breath until you can talk to Justo. Rhys may be in town but I haven't heard anyone say Justo Moro was. Hell, by now he's about reached Agua Prieta, or, an' I'll give you odds on this, or he kept right on going an' won't even look back until he's five miles over the line down into Messico. In his boots that's where I'd be heading."

Matt drained his glass and wagged his head. "It don't make any difference about who drove them barefoot horses. Hell, we got past that part of it before we got down to the goat ranch. It don't even matter about Alba tryin' to double-cross his partners. We got Benton and Hadley, and most important we got back the money. Whoever in hell was also mixed up in the mess is goin' to burrow a deep hole and not even poke his head out for a year or two . . . Tell me something, Sheriff. When a circuit rider gets to town an' holds court, you think you can get Benton and Hadley socked away?"

Harrington was wig-wagging with his empty glass for a re-fill when he answered. "This is a territory not a state. Civil law don't apply. I'm goin' to hold them for the army." Harrington winked. "That was an army payroll they were trying to steal. Matt, if those two see sunlight as free men again for twenty-five years I'll buy you a good horse."

Wales considered that as he too signalled for a refill. Eventually he look quizzically at the lawman. "You know how old I am?"

"No."

"Fifty-six. If you're wrong, if they get out of the stockade within just fifteen years I'd win a horse maybe neither of us'll be above ground to admire, an' even if we're still around, when I'm seventy or thereabouts I won't be ridin' horses . . . You goin' to feed them two or not?"

Matt accompanied the lawman down to the café, helped pack the little pails across the road into the jailhouse, and while Matt took one set of grub buckets to Bryce Hadley, Sheriff Harrington entered the storeroom, where Joshua Benton's rage and rantings had made the place resemble a shambles, and put the other pair of small pails on the floor as he considered the damage. Benton was red-faced, sweaty and dirty. His destructive rampage had stirred dust to life that had probably been dormant in the storeroom for thirty years.

They looked at one another across the devastation when Harrington said, "That's what a child does, Mister Benton. Throws a tantrum. I'm goin' to unlock you and lean against the door until you've put everything back on the shelves or against the walls, and we're not going to say a word to each other while I'm watchin' an' you're cleanin' up."

When the merchant had been freed and was sullenly putting things back to rights, he was silent right up until he looked over and saw Sheriff Harrington regarding him dispassionately, arms crossed over his chest, thick frame against the door, then he spoke.

"Sheriff, it was Hadley's idea."

Harrington woodenly nodded. "Sure it was. He planned the holdup, an' he delivered the gold along with Alba an' maybe Justo. Then Justo busted his buttons gettin' down to town to take Dave Stern's horses out of the public corral and drive them over the tracks of the robbers after he heard them turn into town . . . were you with 'em?"

"Don't be silly, Sheriff."

Harrington accepted that. "All right. But when they turned into town they knew exactly where to go an' you were waiting. Out behind your store at the loading dock? You hid the loot, they had all night to fade away . . . But you'n Hadley had a worry about me inspecting all the freight leaving town, so you waited, and waited, then tried getting it out not by wagon or stage but by mule train . . . Was the third man Justo Moro?"

"Yes. Sheriff, I'll make a swap with you."

"I'll bet you will. You'll throw Alba and Justo to the lions if I'll look the other way for you."

"Better'n that, Sheriff. I'll put three hundred greenbacks under the dock behind the store an' you can leave it there until it's safe for you to recover it."

★ ★ ★

Harrington surveyed the room, decided it was passably orderly again, relocked his upset prisoner into his chains and closed the storeroom door on him. He lighted the office lamp, hung it from its ceiling hook and went down into the cell room where his other prisoner glared.

"Benton says you planned the whole

thing, Bryce. He said it was originally your idea an' that — "

"Lyin' old son of a bitch," snarled Hadley, glaring.

As though there had been no interruption Sheriff Harrington continued speaking. "Accordin' to him it was you came to town ahead of the bullion coach and its guards in the other coaches, looked him up and made the proposition."

Hadley approached the front of the cell wearing a dark scowl. "Does that make any sense to you?" he asked, and looked scornful. "I just rode into town, went directly to the first man I met in the general store and said, 'Let's rob the payroll stage', and he was perfectly agreeable?"

Harrington shrugged and remained silent.

"It was the other way around," Bryce said. "He approached me when I first come to Camargo to scout up the place ahead of the money-coach and its guards."

Harrington looked sceptical. "He just walked up to you and said, 'Let's rob the payroll stage'?"

Hadley's eyes slid to the far wall past Harrington's right shoulder. "I knew him years back. Met him north-west of here at a place called Los Quatros Milpas where I was deputy town marshal. He was delivering Mex gold ornaments, mostly from looted churches, to a little smelter over there. The feller who owned the smelter didn't like it an' came to me. I looked up Mister Benton . . . We had a long talk, an' I told the smelter to go ahead and melt the stuff down."

Harrington smiled at Hadley. "For how much?"

"From Benton? Four hunnert dollars."

Harrington pursed his lips. That was a small fortune on the south desert. He drily said, "I'd say you two knew each other. So — when you came to Camargo?"

"I looked him up, told him what was goin' to happen directly and . . . "

Bryce stopped speaking, continued to gaze out at the sheriff for a while, then turned his back on Harrington and returned to the cot to sit on the edge of it as he finished speaking. "*He* came up with the idea from start to finish."

14

The Return to Normalcy — Sort of

THE following morning Sheriff Harrington was in his office when the watery-eyed clerk from the general store came over looking aggravated. He said customers over yonder were asking all kinds of questions about Mister Benton, and that if Sheriff Harrington didn't release his employer, the store-business was going to go to hell.

Harrington doubted that. Benton's emporium was the only full-service general store within many miles. He told the clerk to make the best of it, and held up his hand when the clerk would have noisily remonstrated. "Mister Benton stays in his cell . . . There's nothin' more to say. I said — *there* — *is* — *nothing*

— *more* — *to* — *say*!"

There would have been something else to discuss if the store clerk had been over at the café earlier when Matt Wales grumblingly confirmed a rumour Harrington had heard, that he had hired out again to the stage company after all manner of towering and grisly oaths that he would never lift a finger for that outfit again as long as he lived.

Matt had also said Evan Rhys, Benton's roustabout, had applied for work at the corralyard and had been hired. At the look he got from Harrington about that, Matt toyed with his coffee cup as he said, "Well, I believe him. I think I believed him down at the water trough. He didn't really know what was goin' on. When he got back to town after bein' untied — him an' the Messican — he was going to look up Mister Benton an' have it out with him . . ."

"And?"

Matt sipped from the cup before

replying. "Well; like he told me at the corralyard this morning — well — Benton has some pretty mean friends, and while Rhys is handy enough an' no coward, like he said, on thinking about it, it seemed to him rather than maybe kill someone or get killed by someone, he'd just cut the cord and begin over."

Harrington did not really care about Rhys. He did care about Alba Moro's brother. Matt had a short answer about Justo. "He left Rhys an' headed for Agua Prieta. That's all Rhys knows." Matt looked quizzically at the lawman. "Where's Patricio? Hell I haven't seen him in two days."

Harrington hadn't either, but, as with Evan Rhys and some other aspects of the recent highway robbery and its after effects, the *arriero's* importance had diminished. All that still mattered was the recovered loot, the pair of men who had engineered the theft, and turning all of it including the loot and the prisoners over to the army.

That is what Sheriff Bruce Harrington thought.

Just short of mid-day two dusty horsemen appeared in Camargo and after overseeing the care of their tired animals, crossed to the café beating off clouds of alkali dust, had a big meal then trudged over to the jailhouse, walked in, nodded to Harrington and sat down. They both wore badges. The older of the pair was Town Marshal Jack Petrie from Agua Prieta. His deputy was Pete Rosson who had a reputation for being a ring-tailed roarer.

Harrington had not seen either of the other lawman in a couple of years. He was sure he knew why they'd made the long ride and offered them coffee before the palavering began.

Marshal Petrie waved the coffee away and got right to business. "We come up here to get your version of what happened at that goat ranch, Sheriff."

Harrington told them in detail. His recitation used up a fair amount of time. Both the marshal and his deputy got cups of coffee before the story was finished and, after it was finished and Marshal Petrie was stirring his java with a thick finger, he spoke without looking up.

"Well; Mister Stern showed up before we left this morning, an' we went out to the Moro place . . . His animals was in the corrals but there was no sign of the Moro boys. We give him his horses, an' because we was comin' up this way anyway, we helped him drive them until all the crackers was out an' they'd settled down to a decent walk, then we cut off for the road. By now I'd guess Mister Stern's got his horses back home."

Harrington was pleased about this but Marshal Petrie continued to stir his coffee without looking up, and that bothered the sheriff a little so he said, "Out with it, Marshal. What're you holdin' back?"

"Well, Sheriff, about them four boys we wrapped in canvas and took back to

Agua Prieta from the goat ranch . . . "

"What about them?"

Marshal Petrie gazed at his deputy and nodded his head. Deputy Marshal Rosson rummaged in a jacket pocket, brought forth a limp small empty Bull Durham sack and tossed it atop the desk. Neither Rosson nor his boss said a word, they sat there waiting for Sheriff Harrington to empty the sack, which he did looking mildly perplexed even after four more or less flattened bullets tumbled atop his desk, and he looked from them to a pair of impassively watching lawmen from Agua Prieta.

The older man said, "Scrape 'em with your pocket knife, Sheriff."

Harrington got out his clasp knife and scraped each bullet a little then placed them side by side and stared at them. For a while the only sound in the office was echoes from beyond the office, out where some lads were chasing a lopsided, discarded steel buggy rim, using sticks to keep it rolling.

Harrington finally let go a loud breath, sat back and looked from the marshal to his deputy. "Where did these come from?" he asked, and got back a reply he half expected.

"From them four fellers we took back to Agua Prieta with us from the goat ranch," Marshal Petrie replied, and leaned forward in the chair. "We took the bodies to our local doctor. He's also the town veterinarian an' undertaker. He removed them bullets from three of them four Mexicans." Petrie eased back in the chair. "Sheriff . . . ?"

Harrington sat back staring at the bullets. He was remembering the aftermath of the fight at the goat ranch when he and Patricio Castillo went searching for the casualties, and his bothersome thoughts as Patricio went unerringly from one corpse to the next — three times.

Marshal Petrie cleared his throat. "Sheriff . . . ?"

"All I can tell you," Harrington said, "is that there was a lot of gunfire. Men were hiding around the yard and for all I know back up the sidehill and beyond the yard. I was in the barn. It wasn't possible to see north or south very well, and with guns goin' off a man'd be an idiot to stick his head out."

That did not satisfy the Agua Prieta lawman. "Sheriff, them bullets was picked out of the men who went up there with Alba Moro. Accordin' to what we heard there was you, a Mex mule-train man and a stage driver in the barn. It was you three against Alba and his five friends. Sheriff: three of them gents was killed by those bullets on your desk. Alba Moro had an everyday forty-five lead slug in him . . . What we'd like to know, Sheriff is — which one of you other gents had those other slugs in your guns . . . Sheriff?"

Harrington roused from his reverie, leaned forward and spoke briskly. "What difference does it make? They tried to highjack a pack train that was carryin' loot from a highway robbery, and four of 'em including Alba, got killed. We got two other men in the cells here in Camargo. Like I told you, they was the ring-leaders. And we got the money back. Marshal, I already explained — there was a lot of shooting going on — "

"We know all that, Sheriff," retorted the town marshal, and levelled a stiff finger in the direction of the desk. "You ever see bullets like that before? I sure never have. Those bullets are pure silver. Now, what we'd like to know is which one of you three fellers uses pure silver instead of lead bullets."

Before Harrington could reply the roadside door opened and Patricio Castillo walked in smiling. No one smiled back so his smile atrophied. He nodded at the strangers before speaking directly to Bruce Harrington. "I got a haul up to Remedios and a haul back. That don't happen very often, full packs both ways. I'll be gone maybe two weeks, I thought I should tell you in case

284

you wanted to see me before I get back."

Harrington nodded woodenly and introduced Castillo by name and occupation, then drily said: "He's the *arriero* who was in the barn with me an' the stage driver down yonder."

The pair of town marshals gazed enquiringly at Castillo. The elder one pointed to the lined-up silver bullets on the desk. "You ever see silver bullets before, *amigo*?"

Patricio's eyes widened as he stepped to the desk, picked up two of the slugs and examined them closely before answering. "*Santa Maria, Señores* . . . they really are silver!" He placed them back in alignment with the others and went to the door where he stopped to look around with widened eyes. "Where did you get them," he said, and before anyone could reply he smiled and rolled his eyes, settled them upon Sheriff Harrington and said: "You know the legend, Sheriff . . . "

"Of *El Matador*?"

"Yes. In the legend *El Matador* uses silver bullets. Even my grandfather told me that. And my father told me too."

Patricio closed the door gently after himself.

Town Marshal Petrie stood up. "I've heard that damned story a dozen times since I been on the south desert. *El Matador*, the big man who rides a black horse, carries fancy guns . . . but I never heard about him using silver slugs before. In fact I never heard of him shootin folks before. Sheriff; let's try an' make some sense out of this. There's no gawddamned Mex Robin Hood goes riding around the country rightin' wrongs."

Harrington shrugged. "You could sure get a lot of hot arguments about that up here in Camargo, Marshal."

"Yeah," stated the man from Agua Prieta drily. "From your Messicans, but —"

"No, not just from our Messicans," stated Harrington and also stood up. "Marshal, I just told you — I was in

286

that barn with two men, Castillo and Matt Wales. I've known them both a lot longer'n I've known you. I'll give you odds of a hunnert to one neither of them owns any silver bullets."

"Well, you also said there was guns goin' off all over the place."

"That's plumb right. Maybe back in the underbrush. Maybe up that northerly sidehill. It sounded like a war for a while."

"Whoa, Sheriff! Are you sayin' this *El Matador* spook was takin' sides down there?"

Harrington went to the roadway door and opened it as he replied: "I'm sayin' Wales, Castillo and I got the money back; got the head Indians that planned the robbery who'll be turned over to the army for prosecution. Old man Stern got his horses back . . . I don't know what happened to Justo Moro, don't give a damn, an' as far as I'm concerned it's over and done with."

Marshal Petrie studied the large man standing beside the opened door, looked at his deputy and jerked his head. As they passed out into sunlight the deputy marshal said, "Sheriff, d'you believe in *fantasmas*?"

"No, sir, Mister Rosson, I sure don't."

"Well, would you mind if we kept them silver slugs?"

Harrington eyed the ring-tailed roarer for a moment before answering. "You a souvenir collector, Deputy?"

"This time I am, Sheriff."

"Take 'em with you. Gents, I want to thank you for ridin' up here today."

Harrington watched them stride southward in the direction of the livery barn, waited until they had turned in down there, then went up to the saloon looking for Matt Wales. He was not at the saloon, he was over at the leather shop again. Harrington took him out front, told him the story of the three silver bullets and waited for the hard-headed scepticism to show. It didn't. Matt fished around in a trouser pocket and dropped a misshapen bullet

288

on the lawman's palm as he said, "I dug this out of a cracked rock five, six years back when some *bandoleros* up over the line stopped my stage on the south road at Point of Rocks."

Harrington's face formed into a mystified scowl. "Border jumpers had silver slugs in their guns?"

"No. They stopped me an' while I was tossin' down the weapons and they come out of the rocks, someone opened up on 'em from farther back. Killed one and the other one got away bellerin' like a wounded eagle. That slug in your hand went through the dead one and stuck in the crack of a big rock. Sterling silver."

"Who fired it?"

Matt made a thin smile. "Hell, I don't know, Sheriff. I never look no gift horses in the mouth. I dragged the dead one out of the road and drove on. Never looked back an' never went back later to snoop around." Matt took back his talisman and pocketed it as he regarded Sheriff Harrington from an expressionless face. "*El Matador?*" he asked quietly. "Naw, you don't believe in crap like that."

Harrington returned his friend's stare. "Patricio was by earlier. He's goin' north with the mules. Might not be back for a couple of weeks."

Matt nodded indifferently. "Glad he got a cargo. Well, me'n the harness maker was going to — "

"Matt, hike over to Mex town with me."

"What for?"

"You know damned well what for. You want to know what I think?"

"Not especially but from the look on your face you're going to tell me anyway."

"I think Patricio's the third generation *El Matador*. I think maybe it started out a hundred years ago as a sort of *patrón* for the Mexicans. They probably needed one worse then than they do now. Anyway, I think Patricio — "

"Sheriff, you said at the café it's over with. You got your prisoners an' the payroll. Is there some special reason you got to keep on worryin' the bone, for Chrissake?"

Harrington halted in mid-stride. They had crossed to the east side of Main Street and were in front of the abstract office. Matt dourly considered the larger man. "Who in hell appointed you solver of the world's mysteries anyway? You got a legal charge against *El Matador*? Did he buck the law? Did he cause trouble? . . . You know what he did, Sheriff? He saved your gawddamned hide at that goat ranch. An' my hide. An' as far as I'm concerned this is as far as I'm goin' with you this morning." Matt abruptly stepped off the duckboards and struck out back the way he had come. Sheriff Harrington watched him all the way, until he disappeared into the harness works, then turned in at the saloon, got a glass of tepid beer, drank it slowly in pensive silence, and when he finally departed he strolled down to Mex town, to the *jacal* of the *arriero*, whom he did not expect to meet, and in fact he didn't meet him. His buxom wife told Harrington her husband had left with the mules about an hour and a half earlier. She also said that if it was very important, Sheriff Harrington could probably overtake her husband on the north stage road, or perhaps a short distance parallel to it, which she said with a smile, was the way he usually travelled.

Harrington was turning away when the handsome woman turned back inside the doorway briefly, then walked out to the edge of the *ramada* holding something in her hand as she called. "*Jefe*! Patricio said to give you this if you came by." As Harrington turned back for the small buckskin wrapped object, the handsome woman also said, "He told me he was sure you would come looking for him today."

Harrington nodded, thanked the woman and pocketed the small package on his way back to the jailhouse. He got waylaid in front of the livery barn by the caféman who had had to chase down one of the light freight outfits that hauled in wholesale supplies for him. He had forgotten to place an order for dried apricots, a delicacy on the south desert. When the lawman came along the caféman was out front, waiting.

He fell in beside Harrington as he said, "Meant to bring this up couple days back but you been a hard man to corner, bein' gone so much and all."

Harrington halted. "Bring what up?"

"Well, Sheriff, I don't like to have to do this, but if you could see what them wholesalers are chargin' me for supplies now you'd understand . . . I got to raise my charge for feedin' prisoners to thirty cents a meal — well, not breakfast, but the other two meals."

Harrington nodded. "I'll let the town council know at the next meeting."

"Sheriff?"

"What."

"Mister Benton's chairman of the council."

Harrington looked blank. "What of it?"

"Bylaws got it that any changes in community services require a vote by the full membership. What I was wondering is — could you hold the meetin' in your cell room? The other members could come, and Mister Benton could cast his vote."

Harrington eyed the caféman for a time without comment. Then waffled. "I don't know about that. Even if the others wouldn't mind I never had anythin' like that at the jailhouse before and — no — I don't think so. But I'll pay the additional fifteen cents for dinner an' supper until Joshua Benton's name can be taken off the council an' a replacement put in his place."

"But Sheriff, why should you pay?"

Harrington smiled. "Because the army'll be along directly to take Benton and Hadley off my hands, an' if I'm real careful I won't arrest no more folks until Benton's replacement can be seated."

Harrington left the caféman gazing after him, resumed his stroll to the jailhouse, walked in, left the door ajar, sat at the desk and carefully unwrapped the little buckskin packet.

It contained one unfired sixgun cartridge. He did not have to scrape the slug to know it was sterling silver. He leaned back in his chair smiling, was still sitting like that when Matt Wales walked in, scarcely more than glanced at the small object amid the litter atop the desk, sank down in the chair beside the door and said, "Well . . . ?"

"Well, what?"

"You went down there and bothered folks."

When Harrington did not immediately reply Matt scowled in his direction, saw the upright bullet, stared at it with his smile fading, and after a time raised his eyes to the lawman's face. "Where'd you get it?" he asked.

"From Patricio's wife. He left it for her to give to me after he went up the road with his mules."

Matt leaned to make a closer inspection. Before settling back he asked another question. "Why?"

Harrington employed Castillo's tactic; he shrugged without speaking.

The stage driver sat a while looking gravely at the scuffed toes of his old boots, then brightened a little. "That makes five, don't it?"

"Yep."

"He didn't break no law, did he?"

"Nope."

"Then you got no call to trouble him, have you?"

"Nope."

Matt continued to consider his boots. "Then what's your position?"

"Like you said at the café, Matt, it's over. The money's safe, the bastards who tried to steal it are locked up, and that's the end of it."

"I mean about *El Matador*."

"I don't know anythin' about *El Matador*. He's a Mex town legend, that's all I know. It's said he rides through down there once in a long

296

while an' tosses gold coins through folks's windows. . . . I don't see anythin' wrong with that. Whether it really happens or not, I don't see anythin' wrong with it."

Matt was rising from his chair when two men in dusty blue uniforms walked in out of the sunlight. They were from the Fort Dix administration unit which was closer to the border and eastward about sixty-five miles. They had come in response to a letter stating that a stolen army payroll had been recovered and that two of the thieves were in the Camargo jailhouse.

As Harrington introduced himself and Matt Wales, and hands were shaken, one of the officers, a man with a dusting of grey at the temples, held out his left hand palm upward.

Harrington and Wales stared. The officer was holding an unfired sixgun cartridge. "We came down the north roadway early this morning. Captain Jefferson here thinks he saw a large man come out of the underbrush on the east side of the road, lean and place something in the middle of the road, then raise up, look toward us, and go back into the underbrush . . . That was in the middle of the road. A silver bullet."

Harrington looked at Matt. "Six," he said. Wales gravely inclined his head. The officers looked from one of them to the other before the senior officer said, "Six? Does this have anything to do with the payroll robbery?"

Harrington took the bullet, pocketed it as he smilingly wagged his head. "Don't have a thing to do with it, now if you gents'll have a seat I'll bring out your prisoners? You got horses to take them back on, and irons?"

"We have a prison wagon. It's down at the livery barn."

"I'll fetch your prisoners, gents."

After the sheriff had left the room one of the officers asked Matt Wales if there was a significance to the silver bullet, and Matt, who was never very expressive in the face under the best

— or worst — of circumstances blandly shook his head. "Don't mean a thing, gents, except that we got an old legend down here about a mysterious feller who rides a big black horse and goes through Mex town every once in a while tossin' coins at folks."

"Does that have anything to do with the silver bullet?" the senior officer asked, and Matt shook his head. "Nope. Maybe someone likes to keep the old legend alive and let you gents find one of them slugs. It wouldn't hurt any to have genuine army officers tell around town that they found a silver bullet. Sort of keep the legend alive."

The senior officer responded drily. "The army doesn't deal in legends, Mister Wales. In fact as far as the army's concerned, legends in this country are a cause for a lot of hard riding and wasted time. I've been on the border thirteen years and not once in all that time have I found any basis in fact for local damned superstitions."

Matt agreed heartily just before he

departed, leaving the soldiers in the jailhouse office. "Me neither, gents, an' I been here more'n thirteen years. Have a nice trip back."

THE END

Other titles in the Linford Western Library:

TOP HAND
Wade Everett

The Broken T was big. But no ranch is big enough to let a man hide from himself.

GUN WOLVES OF LOBO BASIN
Lee Floren

The Feud was a blood debt. When Smoke Talbot found the outlaws who gunned down his folks he aimed to nail their hide to the barn door.

SHOTGUN SHARKEY
Marshall Grover

The westbound coach carrying the indomitable Larry and Stretch headed for a shooting showdown.

FIGHTING RAMROD
Charles N. Heckelmann

Most men would have cut their losses, but Frazer counted the bullets in his guns and said he'd soak the range in blood before he'd give up another inch of what was his.

LONE GUN
Eric Allen

Smoke Blackbird had been away too long. The Lequires had seized the Blackbird farm, forcing the Indians and settlers off, and no one seemed willing to fight! He had to fight alone.

THE THIRD RIDER
Barry Cord

Mel Rawlins wasn't going to let anything stand in his way. His father was murdered, his two brothers gone. Now Mel rode for vengeance.

ARIZONA DRIFTERS
W. C. Tuttle

When drifting Dutton and Lonnie Steelman decide to become partners they find that they have a common enemy in the formidable Thurston brothers.

TOMBSTONE
Matt Braun

Wells Fargo paid Luke Starbuck to outgun the silver-thieving stagecoach gang at Tombstone. Before long Luke can see the only thing bearing fruit in this eldorado will be the gallows tree.

HIGH BORDER RIDERS
Lee Floren

Buckshot McKee and Tortilla Joe cut the trail of a border tough who was running Mexican beef into Texas. They stopped the smuggler in his tracks.

BRETT RANDALL, GAMBLER
E. B. Mann

Larry Day had the choice of running away from the law or of assuming a dead man's place. No matter what he decided he was bound to end up dead.

THE GUNSHARP
William R. Cox

The Eggerleys weren't very smart. They trained their sights on Will Carney and Arizona's biggest blood bath began.

THE DEPUTY OF SAN RIANO
Lawrence A. Keating and
Al. P. Nelson

When a man fell dead from his horse, Ed Grant was spotted riding away from the scene. The deputy sheriff rode out after him and came up against everything from gunfire to dynamite.

FARGO: MASSACRE RIVER
John Benteen

The ambushers up ahead had now blocked the road. Fargo's convoy was a jumble, a perfect target for the insurgents' weapons!

SUNDANCE: DEATH IN THE LAVA
John Benteen

The Modoc's captured the wagon train and its cargo of gold. But now the halfbreed they called Sundance was going after it . . .

HARSH RECKONING
Phil Ketchum

Five years of keeping himself alive in a brutal prison had made Brand tough and careless about who he gunned down . . .

FARGO: PANAMA GOLD
John Benteen

With foreign money behind him, Buckner was going to destroy the Panama Canal before it could be completed. Fargo's job was to stop Buckner.

FARGO:
THE SHARPSHOOTERS
John Benteen

The Canfield clan, thirty strong were raising hell in Texas. Fargo was tough enough to hold his own against the whole clan.

PISTOL LAW
Paul Evan Lehman

Lance Jones came back to Mustang for just one thing — revenge! Revenge on the people who had him thrown in jail.

HELL RIDERS
Steve Mensing

Wade Walker's kid brother, Duane, was locked up in the Silver City jail facing a rope at dawn. Wade was a ruthless outlaw, but he was smart, and he had vowed to have his brother out of jail before morning!

DESERT OF THE DAMNED
Nelson Nye

The law was after him for the murder of a marshal — a murder he didn't commit. Breen was after him for revenge — and Breen wouldn't stop at anything . . . blackmail, a frameup . . . or murder.

DAY OF THE COMANCHEROS
Steven C. Lawrence

Their very name struck terror into men's hearts — the Comancheros, a savage army of cutthroats who swept across Texas, leaving behind a bloodstained trail of robbery and murder.

SUNDANCE: SILENT ENEMY
John Benteen

A lone crazed Cheyenne was on a personal war path. They needed to pit one man against one crazed Indian. That man was Sundance.

LASSITER
Jack Slade

Lassiter wasn't the kind of man to listen to reason. Cross him once and he'll hold a grudge for years to come — if he let you live that long.

LAST STAGE TO GOMORRAH
Barry Cord

Jeff Carter, tough ex-riverboat gambler, now had himself a horse ranch that kept him free from gunfights and card games. Until Sturvesant of Wells Fargo showed up.

McALLISTER ON THE COMANCHE CROSSING
Matt Chisholm

The Comanche, McAllister owes them a life — and the trail is soaked with the blood of the men who had tried to outrun them before.

QUICK-TRIGGER COUNTRY
Clem Colt

Turkey Red hooked up with Curly Bill Graham's outlaw crew. But wholesale murder was out of Turk's line, so when range war flared he bucked the whole border gang alone . . .

CAMPAIGNING
Jim Miller

Ambushed on the Santa Fe trail, Sean Callahan is saved by two Indian strangers. But there'll be more lead and arrows flying before the band join Kit Carson against the Comanches.

GUNSLINGER'S RANGE
Jackson Cole

Three escaped convicts are out for revenge. They won't rest until they put a bullet through the head of the dirty snake who locked them behind bars.

RUSTLER'S TRAIL
Lee Floren

Jim Carlin knew he would have to stand up and fight because he had staked his claim right in the middle of Big Ike Outland's best grass.

THE TRUTH ABOUT SNAKE RIDGE
Marshall Grover

The troubleshooters came to San Cristobal to help the needy. For Larry and Stretch the turmoil began with a brawl and then an ambush.

WOLF DOG RANGE
Lee Floren

Will Ardery would stop at nothing, unless something stopped him first — like a bullet from Pete Manly's gun.

DEVIL'S DINERO
Marshall Grover

Plagued by remorse, a rich old reprobate hired the Texas Troubleshooters to deliver a fortune in greenbacks to each of his victims.

GUNS OF FURY
Ernest Haycox

Dane Starr, alias Dan Smith, wanted to close the door on his past and hang up his guns, but people wouldn't let him.

DONOVAN
Elmer Kelton

Donovan was supposed to be dead. Uncle Joe Vickers had fired off both barrels of a shotgun into the vicious outlaw's face as he was escaping from jail. Now Uncle Joe had been shot — in just the same way.

CODE OF THE GUN
Gordon D. Shirreffs

MacLean came riding home, with saddle tramp written all over him, but sewn in his shirt-lining was an Arizona Ranger's star.

GAMBLER'S GUN LUCK
Brett Austen

Gamblers seldom live long. Parker was a hell of a gambler. It was his life — or his death . . .

ORPHAN'S PREFERRED
Jim Miller

Sean Callahan answers the call of the Pony Express and fights Indians and outlaws to get the mail through.

DAY OF THE BUZZARD
T. V. Olsen

All Val Penmark cared about was getting the men who killed his wife.

THE MANHUNTER
Gordon D. Shirreffs

Lee Kershaw knew that every Rurale in the territory was on the lookout for him. But the offer of $5,000 in gold to find five small pieces of leather was too good to turn down.

RIFLES ON THE RANGE

Doc Mike and the farmer stood there alone between Smith and Watson. There was this moment of stillness, and then the roar would start. And somebody would die . . .

HARTIGAN
Marshall Grover

Hartigan had come to Cornerstone to die. He chose the time and the place, and Main Street became a battlefield.

SUNDANCE: OVERKILL
John Benteen

When a wealthy banker's daughter was kidnapped by the Cheyenne, he offered Sundance $10,000 to rescue the girl.